The Exquisite Chemistry of Blood

ISBN-13: 9781680630022
USBN-10: 1680630024

Cover Image: AnnyM | 99Designs.com

Published by
Myrddin Publishing
Contact us at myrddinpublishing.com

unique electronic & print books

THE EXQUISITE CHEMISTRY OF BLOOD

ALISON DELUCA

For Genna

"Nature is a haunted house –
but Art –
is a house that tries to be haunted."
EMILY DICKINSON

• • •

"I am a great admirer of mystery and magic.
Look at this life – all mystery and magic."
HARRY HOUDINI

THE EXQUISITE CHEMISTRY OF BLOOD

ALISON DELUCA

PART I
STARTER'S PISTOL

CHAPTER 1.

Julia stands in a triangle of Blue Anchor's park, balancing a small house made of balsa and plastic on her left hip. Its sharp edges dig into her skin.

"Things are about to happen," Ghost declares. "I can sense it in the alignment of planets, or maybe it's a strange mix of chemistry. It makes me feel twitchy."

"Good or bad things?" Julia asks.

Ghost doesn't answer.

The cheap mass-produced little house is Julia's most precious possession. In a few weeks it will be the first Little Free Library in Blue Anchor, the New Jersey town where she lives. Anyone will be able to take a book from the shelves hidden inside and, if they like, leave one behind for future readers.

Julia strokes the underside, and a splinter slides into the pad of her ring finger. She's worked her ass off to get this far, and she refuses to let Ghost's mysterious 'things' get in her way.

Even if she feels twitchy, whatever that means.

• • •

Bash slams on the brakes. His sudden stop makes the bottles of amber liquor clink and roll underneath the passenger seat and Bash knows he shouldn't drive so fast, not with all that alcohol hidden in his car.

His to-do list includes homework, Harley, and a mile-long list of chores, but he won't finish before midnight. Nehi, as usual, has sucked up all his time and energy.

If only he could...

Bash doesn't know the end of that sentence. If only he could – what? Run away? Get out of Jersey, hop on a train? He knows how to use his grandfather's woodworking tools, enough to talk his way into an internship at a shop somewhere.

But it's not an option. The mere existence of Nehi makes any plans impossible.

The Dart's engine stutters and shudders as, under the passenger seat, the bottles rattle together in an infuriating rhythm. Bash twists sideways to drag an old drop cloth from the backseat and drapes it over his booze cache, gritting his teeth. If he does get pulled over, the last thing he needs is a curious cop searching the Dart's interior.

The red light where he's stopped stares down like a single, smug eyeball. Bash is so anxious to step on the gas and get going he doesn't notice the car in the lane next to him until the occupant taps the horn and startles him out of his thoughts.

Not a cop. Bash feels relief ice his veins.

A girl has pulled up in her sparkly new SUV next to the Dart. She's pretty, blond, with a big smile. For a second he thinks London has followed him.

The girl shouts a question at him. It's not London – she would never do such a thing. London gives orders, not questions.

"What?" Bash winds down the manual window. "What do you want?" It's rude, but he doesn't care.

"I said you're cute. Doing anything later?" the girl repeats. She's desperate enough to chase thrills at a stoplight on a Thursday night.

Is that a siren in the distance? An ambulance? A police car?

"Sorry," Bash tells her. He jams his work boot on the accelerator just as the light turns green and squeals forward, forcing the Dart to go from zero to a shuddery fifty mph. The old car whines, sulky as a spoiled debutante, grudgingly going into third gear.

A physics lesson from tenth grade comes back to Bash as he leans forward, both hands on the wheel. Acceleration is the change of velocity of an object over time, with v as the final speed and u as the starting point. T is the time elapsed: $v = u + at$. The neat formula doesn't consider the age of the Dart, what type of engine oil Bash can afford, or the number of hours he spends on the old engine to keep the car running. And which

CHAPTER 1.

variables stand for desperation, for cheap whiskey, for the amount of rye already drunk from the bottle?

He knows the science behind that process, how alcohol is metabolized quickly in the bloodstream. It's sent straight to the brain and soft tissues via a chemical interaction and brings quick mercy, a way to forget, tender amnesia for someone who's seen too much.

Rolled out of the factory in 1970, his Dodge Dart has half the trunk space of the 1969 model and an 8-cylinder automatic transmission. Bash drives a Swinger, the 2-door model. Its reduced seat and trunk space give the engine less drag, so by pounding on the gas pedal he's able to lose the blond and that wailing siren.

Bash breathes through pursed lips as he turns into a park system, Blue Anchor's latest construction. He's studied the map of the streets there, laid out like veins that branch from the main soccer fields and branch to the dog park, hiking trails, and forest walks – places where people can do private crimes.

He rolls up the window with an ancient hand-crank that has disappeared from new car technology. The glass reflects his face: messy black hair grown long enough to cover his neck, flat nose, wide mouth, shadowed eyes under stormy brows.

The Dart winds through the park, and in the solitude Bash finally lets himself relax against his car's scratchy upholstery. The soccer fields disappear and are replaced with clumps of pines bisected with bike paths. He's certain he's alone there, since the darkness is spiked only by an occasional streetlamp.

There he stops the car and cracks open the door. The silence is complete, since the soccer players and their cheering parents have all gone home, but still he waits and forces himself to count to one thousand before proceeding.

The tarp crackles as Bash pulls it back to reveal the bottles. He selects one filled with vodka, emblazoned with an improbable Russian name and half-filled with clear liquid. Around him, the trees and streets seem to wait.

He doesn't have much time left. Bash lets out a long whoosh of breath and unscrews the lid.

• • •

"It looks good," Ghost says.

Julia pushes back her red curls. The little bookshelf is her personal triumph, erected in defiance of Blue Anchor's suspicious local government. Even the mayor put forth a self-righteous list of concerns at one of the township meetings, but with hard work Julia managed to get a sympathetic majority on her side to fund her very own Little Free Library in the town park.

This belongs to her and Ghost, no one else.

In order to bypass a lot of red tape, she has to put up the house after hours or lose her hard-won temporary construction permit for public lands. It's why she's here in the shadowy park when most kids are out with friends or doing homework.

She's filed for those permits, held fundraisers, even written to her dead mom's favorite author, Hillman Minx. His publicist, D. Craniver, has written back. After a long series of negotiations, Julia has secured a tentative arrangement to present a signed copy of *A Change of Velocity* at the Little Free Library opening in a few weeks.

The actual library is tiny, the cheapest model on the Little Free Library website and all Julia could afford. "It's fine," Ghost comments. "I can work with it, make the inside all calm and comfy."

Too intent on her project, Julia doesn't bother to ask what Ghost means by that. The books will go inside the top section of the tiny house, a donation to any reader who wants them. Julia eyes the sharpened end of the post, wondering if she can get it into the ground securely when the time comes. This is why she's trying it out afterhours in the park and weeks before the library is actually installed.

But the ground is loose and gives easily. It just takes a few pushes and some mumbled curses to set the little library upright.

Julia steps back and regards her achievement. She has spent hours after school collecting books from her friends, her friends' friends, from parents and teachers and strangers. Homework assignments have been pushed aside as she sorted and rejected titles to make certain the Little Free Library would open with the best possible selection of novels and nonfiction. Her grades have suffered more than usual as a result, and she doesn't even want to think about Fry's upcoming chemistry paper.

"Why would a chemistry teacher assign an essay, anyway?" she mutters. It's such a stupid assignment: *Describe how chemistry affects your everyday life.*

All the chemistry in the world couldn't help when a drunk driver hit her mom's car. He walked away without a scratch while Julia's mother bled out on a gurney.

She didn't even survive the ambulance ride to the ER.

With careful fingers, Julia traces the hinged door of the library. It's constructed of plain wood designed for utility rather than beauty. In order to see the titles inside, future readers will have to open the door. There are weatherproofed models with glass windows, but Julia couldn't afford them.

"But what is it?" her dad asked when she first told him about the project. "I never heard of such a thing."

"The libraries are miniature houses. People all over the world put them up. The concept is for readers to show up, take a book and leave another in its place if they can." Julia remembers following him around the kitchen as he chopped vegetables and threw them into a pot. "This would be the first one in Blue Anchor," she explained. "I just thought Mom would have liked it."

He made an excuse to leave the room after that.

Julia wonders what it will look like with actual books inside, the ones she has stashed inside her truck. She peers down the silent park road, wondering if she should chance putting a few hardbacks on the shelf.

No reason not to try it out. She's alone, after all.

"Hey! I'm still here," Ghost reminds her.

"Shh. If someone drives by, they'll see a crazy redhead talking to herself." Julia walks to the truck, climbs into the truck bed, and folds back the lid of one carton. *House on Mango Street*, *eleanor & park*, and *The Life of Pi* snuggle up to *Jane Eyre*, *Madame Bovary*, and *The Wizard of Oz*. She shoves the phone in her back pocket and selects *A Change of Velocity*.

"My favorite," Ghost says.

As she jumps down from the truck, Julia hears the unmistakable Doppler whine of an approaching car. *Rattle*, she thinks. *Shaky engine.* She's well acquainted with those sounds, since her truck is also ancient.

The vehicle blasts into view, fuzzy in the darkness. Fast enough to shock Julia into paralysis, the car speeds towards them and its front fender clips the sidewalk with a harsh bark. It's followed by a loud Bang! as Julia's Little Free Library explodes over the hood of the car and rattles onto the ground in pieces.

Never hesitating, the driver and car disappear into the darkness of the park's drive. All that is left is its trail of destruction: tire tracks like huge gashes in the grass sprinkled with wood and plastic confetti, the fragments of Julia's carefully curated little library house.

There's no sudden brake, no concern, no question of "Oh my gosh, are you okay?" or "Hey, wow, I'm so sorry that happened, I'm such a bonehead. Let me pay for the damage."

Ghost leaps to her feet and shakes one fist in the direction of the car. "Come back here and fight me, you dirty filthy disgusting... *road hog!*"

Julia is frozen beside her truck, still clutching *A Change of Velocity*. The disaster has occurred so quickly she hasn't had time to take out her phone and record the license plate before the car that destroyed all her hard work disappears. There hasn't even been enough time to see the make or color in the gathering dark.

Car.

Driver.

Her Little Free Library.

All gone.

"No no no no no." Julia drops the books and runs to the wreckage of the tiny house. Maybe she can turn back time or make everything right again with enough denial. "No. That did not just happen. Please, please tell me that didn't happen and everything's okay again, just please could you tell me that?"

With no other recourse, she tips back her head and screams at the stars. They don't seem to mind. The faraway suns twinkle back at her in cold, alien understanding.

• • •

At home Julia parks by their tilted mailbox and opens the rusting door. Inside are the usual sheaf of bills, which she'll pay later from her dad's diminishing account. It's been funding them for over a year after she deposited her mom's life insurance payout.

When the money's gone, Julia has no idea what they'll do. She'll probably have to look for another job – but how can a 17-year-old pay the mortgage?

She'll just have to make it happen. They don't have another choice.

"Sorry, kid." Ghost pulls Julia in for a quick hug. "Might as well go in and face him."

The garage door closes with a squeak. Julia trails through the mudroom into the kitchen where Tom, Julia's dad, waves a vegetable peeler and scatters vegetable skins like orange confetti over the kitchen counter. "Do you like carrot soup?" he demands without preamble. His clothes always appear too small for such a large man. Both wrists, heavy with hair and muscle, are strangled in his tight shirt cuffs.

Tom keeps his lace-up leather shoes on even though he's at home. Each morning he polishes them with a tin of Kiwi and an old rag, although he doesn't have a job. Julia's never seen him in sneakers or sweatpants, always sharply ironed workpants and collared shirts.

She peers at his huge pile of peeled carrots. "Carrot soup. Ugh. I never heard of such a thing."

His mouth bunches up under his nose. "Well, you could…" He doesn't finish his thought.

When she joins him at the sink, he throws out an arm and pulls her into his white shirt which smells like onions. "Gonna bring a bowl to Mom," he murmurs into Julia's hair. "She might even eat it this time. Don't you think?"

Julia pushes away from her dad and leans on the counter. They stare at each other under the buzzing kitchen light where another moth has been lured inside the glass globe. She can hear the creature's frantic wings beating against the etched surface as she searches for words, tries and discards several statements before deciding on the easiest thing to say. "Sure. Why not."

His eyes slip away from her like hardboiled eggs kept in a metal bowl. The kitchen is warm, filled with the sounds of the dying moth and the muffled clunk of his spoon against the battered soup pot.

"How did everything go?" Dad's voice gives out and he has to clear his throat. "In the park, I mean. Your project all squared away?"

"Well, no actually." Julia picks up one of the carrots and bites into it. It's cold against her teeth. "You won't believe this. As soon as I put up the Little Free Library, a car zoomed out of nowhere and hit the box. Wreckage all over the place, serious carnage. The asshole driver just kept going, too."

The spoon drops out of Dad's fingers with an orange splash. "What? You worked so hard on it for Mom. I mean, you wanted to get her favorite book in there…"

"It's not going to happen now." Julia is still trying to take in the fact that some bastard has obliterated her mom's library. "Got the pieces in the truck." Without much hope, she adds, "Want to come into the garage with me and see?"

"Well. Soup first. Maybe later." Her dad slaps the lid on the pot. "Should be ready in an hour. Time for your homework while we wait."

She ducks her head. Is the chemistry book even in her backpack? Julia pulls her bag onto the table, jerks open the grumpy zip, and rustles through the contents.

No book. In her mission to put up the Library, she's forgotten the textbook and will have to rely on her sketchy notes to study for the test.

Fantastic. Her least favorite subject just got worse.

Julia struggles through scrawled pages and reads incomplete phrases about concepts she doesn't understand. While she studies, Tom slices bread and gets out a tray, lining it with a yellowed napkin embroidered with poppies and forget-me-nots. Her mom made it years ago.

"Poked my finger about fifty thousand times embroidering that stupid thing," Ghost whispers into Julia's hair. "There are so many other better hobbies, like arguing on 4chan or flinging yourself off a cliff."

Her dad carefully aligns the cloth and puts buttered bread on a small plate before holding it out. "Ready," he says.

Julia puts down her pen, stands, and slouches to the little bay window over the sink. The screen is ripped through enough for her to slide open the pane and pluck a Nelly Moser blossom from the clematis vine growing wild outside.

• • •

Her parents' room is stuck in time without moths, bubbling carrot soup, or any sounds at all. The only occupant is a motionless lump in the bed.

Julia holds her breath and puts the tray on the little bedside table. Although the curtains are closed, a rogue slice of moon carves into the dusty surface of a full-length mirror, the scarred wood floor, and an oak tallboy. The lump in the bed doesn't stir when Julia leans on one corner of the mattress and leans over.

Carefully she adjusts the long pillows under the blankets and arranges them to look as though a person sleeps in the silent space. The bedroom has been empty for nearly a year. No one else sleeps there anymore, not since Dad moved to the couch and later into their tiny laundry room.

Julia shivers. An impulse sends her to the low bookshelf under the windows, since her father will get all weird if she comes out too quickly.

Mom's old version of *A Change in Velocity* is on the end, shrouded in a waxy envelope.

The paper crinkles under Julia's fingertips as she lifts the flap and removes the book. It's a flimsy paperback first-edition, published before anyone knew Hillman Minx would go viral and become a sensation. Under the title, Wilma Rudolph's beautiful profile gazes serenely off to the left, content to look for a finish line no one else can see.

"He saw her as a whole person," Ghost points out. She tends to become serious and lose her streak of wicked humor when talking about the Velocity book. "It wasn't all about overcoming polio, although that was important too. Wilma made mistakes and still soared into history. Plus, she was a serious badass."

In the bed, the lumpy pillows seem to wait as Julia slides the book back into its envelope and replaces it on the shelf. Later, she'll return and get the untouched tray. Bread will go in the garbage. The soup will sluice into their old garbage disposal, bright orange in the scarred porcelain sink.

"This is barbaric." Ghost shudders. "Pillows, really? Like I'm a boy who sneaks out to go fishing. And I never stayed still, *especially* in bed."

"Ugh," Julia groans. "Really? That's the very last thing I want to imagine."

Ghost just laughs. "Come on, let's get the hell out of here."

• • •

Friday morning brings guilt, coffee, and stolen moments of homework on the way to school. Julia rescues the chemistry text from her messy locker and sneaks it into class for some last-minute studying until the Lit teacher catches her.

When it's time to go to chemistry class, Julia has worked herself into full-blown panic. She considers going to the nurse for an early dismissal, but she's used her Dead Parent card too many times over the past few months.

Swallowing, Julia goes into the class and takes her usual seat. The quiet guy next to her passes over the test papers, and she considers that she doesn't know anything about him. His handwriting is neat, his name in block capitals as he prints it on his copy of the test: BASH.

When Julia looks at her own paper, it's worse than she thought. Mr. Fry's test on the properties and groups of the Periodic Table might as well be in Ancient Sumerian or Mayan glyphs. No mention of blood, which Julia knows is composed of oxygen, carbon dioxide, and nitrogen as well as plasma proteins and H Two fucking Oh.

A fretful, sweaty interlude passes. Bash works steadily, thick brows bunched together and murder in his brown eyes. Across their group's lab table, London clicks shut her pen, sets it in the center of her down-turned test, and holds up her blinged-out phone. A whippet-thin blonde, the girl spends most of the class texting. Mr. Fry, who's usually on top of the rules, lets her get away with it.

"Time," Mr. Fry states. Julia's paper is smudged and wrinkled from her errors, and she blinks back frustration. London's test looks untouched. As for Bash, he folds his into a neat square with the corners lined up perfectly.

"The significance of the number 28." Mr. Fry stops beside Julia's chair and points his reading glasses in her direction. "Can you tell me what that is?"

Bewildered by her failure and the little library's destruction, Julia says, "The atomic number of nickel." She knows that much. Ghost goes over the Periodic Table of Elements with her at night when Julia can't sleep.

"Impressive." The teacher strides to the white board and picks up a red marker. "However, it's also the number of days you have left before your papers are due." He writes the 2 and 8 inside a circle to the background of groans.

London taps one oval nail on the group table. "Bash. Hitting Isaac's party tonight? Isaac might puke down the back of the refrigerator again. Come with me and have fun for once." Her bright gaze is intent on his face.

Bash seems fascinated by another of his paper squares. "I know parties aren't your thing," London adds, tipping forward in her seat. "But Jake's out of town and I just can't stay home in the empty house one more night."

He ignores her and pushes his paper square into the back pocket of his pants. London sucks her teeth and scowls at Julia. "You. Yeah, you," she adds in an annoyed tone when Julia jumps. "Want to go to a party tonight?"

• • •

Julia opens the back door of what is apparently Isaac's house and peers inside the crowded kitchen. Red Solo cups are everywhere – lined up on counters, clustered over the island and table, in the hands of kids talking over the loud music.

The party is filled with the usual sweat and determined revelry of a high school beer bash. Julia's been to a few, got sick at one and danced on the table at another. She met Harry when she fell off the furniture. They hooked up, even dated for a few months until she got sick of his infidelity.

"You need a drink." A kid with blond hair spiked in careful disarray hands a cup to Julia and produces a bottle. With a flourish he breaks the seal and pours something blue over the ice in her glass. "I'm pretty sure it's turpentine, so don't thank me just yet."

Julia sips and grimaces. "That's just nasty."

His grin is unrepentant. "Gets the job done, though."

"Do you go to Blue Anchor High?" Julia takes another cautious sip.

"Nope, I already did my time in jail. Uh, who are you again? And do you wanna dance?"

Julia introduces herself, asks his name. He's Isaac, the guy throwing the party. His smile is infectious when he twirls her into his chest, spins her out in a graceful circle, lets her go to jump into another conversation.

"Don't waste your time with him," someone says in Julia's ear.

She tilts her head. London is standing there with a cup in her hand.

"You mean Isaac?"

"Yeah." London takes a drink and wrinkles her nose.

"Okay." Julia really doesn't want to get into it. "I'm not interested, he just gave me a drink."

London blinks as if she's considering Julia's answer and seems to come to the decision that the whole incident is beneath her. Without another word she disappears into the crowd, her slender and confident figure parting the waves of drunk boys. Already London's got her phone out, tapping out a message with one thumb. Maybe she's texting Bash to tell him to hurry up and join her.

"Woah. Rude. It's obvious she wants nothing more to do with you, so why the invite?" Ghost murmurs.

Who knows. London might have hidden layers, as hidden and mysterious as a complex formula.

Isaac has been drafted by the usual pack of males building a beer can tower. Julia recognizes a few of them – the two tall guys in matching lacrosse jackets sit at the next table in her Chem class. On the sidelines a guy arm-wrestles a girl, and he smacks down her fist with a crow of triumph.

Beer-chugging contests are going on all over the place, and one guy in a button-down shirt laughs as he holds up a selfie stick. On the couch a boy shotguns a joint into a girl's mouth and mixes the smoke with dopey kisses.

The scene's familiar, a replay of most of the parties Julia's attended. She could forget the Little Free Library project and actually be a normal girl, flirt and dance and get wasted by midnight, but no one else at the party has a ghost for a best friend. Time to escape.

There's a huge farmhouse sink in the massive kitchen. Of course no one's looking at her, so Julia pours the Solo cup turpentine down the drain and rinses away the blue, sugary liquid before sidling to the back door.

"You're not allowed to leave." Isaac appears at Julia's side just as she's about to sneak out.

The entire evening has been a waste of time. Isaac's pupils are dilated, and London has disappeared. "Work," Julia says vaguely, waving one hand in the air. "Got stuff to do."

"No, you can't go. If you leave now, I'll know it's because you're having a terrible time and I'll have failed today's goal of throwing an epic party. Please stay?"

She can smell alcohol on his breath. "I had a great time," Julia lies. "Awesome drinks, good company…"

"You're a terrible liar."

"No, I'm a great liar."

"At least just play me in Mario Kart before you go." Isaac's blond spikes brush her shoulder as he leans in to plead with her. She can feel his warm breath on her skin. "One game, I promise. Then you can leave and I won't say a word."

Julia remembers the careful pillows in the silent bedroom at home. She might as well do something normal.

Isaac grins, grabs her hand, and heads towards a flight of stairs. He doesn't acknowledge the group of guys on the landing, beers in hand, who cheer on two girls making out on the steps.

Julia is towed down to a luxuriously finished basement, complete with wet bar on one side and a huge media center. "Sorry about the designer show-room furniture," he says. The place has dark wood floors partially covered by thick area carpets in crimson and gold. Julia plops on one of the couches, squishing into the soft yellow leather.

It's quieter away from the main party. Isaac fumbles in a drawer on the coffee table and mutters something about batteries for his controllers before sliding onto the floor and putting his chin on Julia's knee. "This is good," he says. "Just wanted to hang out and chill for a while."

"So why invite all those people?" Julia asks. "You could have had a few close friends over instead of trashing your house."

"I want to get back at my family. They don't like my life choices."

"Oh yeah?"

"Yeah," Isaac says. He doesn't explain, and Julia doesn't ask. Instead he picks his character, Princess Peach, and sets up a race on the jittery track.

It's relaxing to sit on yellow leather and play a mindless video game. The past few months have been a long grind as she raised funds and stood in line for permits, wrote countless proposals for those damn bakes sales.

Julia wins the first round, and Isaac high-fives her. "Do you know Vincent?" he asks.

"Who now?"

"Just wondering how you heard about the party. How about London? You know her?"

"Oh. Yeah." Julia twists her controller. "She's the one who told me about tonight. Friend of yours?"

Isaac grunts. "I guess. We hung out a few times."

Hanging out, in Julia's experience, means booty calls and quick hook-ups. She can't imagine London and Isaac together, but stranger things have happened. In any case, she doesn't care. The most important thing besides getting her life together, is figuring out how to deal with the destruction of that Little Free Library.

On the screen, her character crashes over the edge of a cliff.

• • •

Julia leaves before midnight. The house is on its way to being completely trashed, and the crowd of guests has doubled. When Isaac leads kneels down to offer her his hand in marriage, Julia knows it's time to go.

The darkness makes it difficult to find her truck. Isaac's yard seems as large as a mall parking lot, and she nearly bumps into a guy and girl at the end of the long front walk.

Ghost elbows Julia and raises one finger to her lips.

"You finally got here." London stands on tiptoe and slips her arms around Bash's neck, a beautiful and balletic move.

"And *you* shouldn't drive." His voice is low and husky. "I'm taking you home."

CHAPTER 2.

When Julia walks into chemistry class on Monday, London is already at the table glaring at her phone. "Oh, no way. Not going to happen." Her thumb ring taps on the screen as she texts in a rapid, annoyed rhythm. "Bash, do you see this crap?"

"Hold on," he grunts. "Just checking on Nehi."

Julia dumps her backpack on the scuffed floor tiles, and London looks up. "Oh, hey. Guess you survived the carnage. I was so hung-over on Saturday, ugh."

"Isaac's a character." Julia pulls out her notebook and pen. "Known him long?"

"Shh." London points to the front of the class where Mr. Fry writes a new number in the red circle: 25. "Keep working on your papers," he states. "I want a multi-layered approach to how chemistry affects your life. Make sure you've paid attention to all the course materials, of course, and if you can include new research you'll make me happy."

"Multi-layered approach." London nudges Julia. Her smile reveals one snagged incisor. "What does that even mean?"

"Maybe Mr. Fry wants examples from real life," Julia guesses. A vision of her mom's room with its humped pillows and cold soup makes her shiver. Where does silence fit on Mr. Fry's periodic table? How about agoraphobia? How about a speeding car that explodes someone into blood and bone – where does that go on the chart of elements?

"Real life. Huh. You actually just gave me an idea." London taps on her phone and slides it across the table to Julia. There's a single demand on the girl's Notes app: *Your Number*.

London isn't the usual kind of person Julia usually hangs with, unlike the waitresses at the diner, her dad, Isaac from the other night, and D. Craniver. Her top contact is the unpleasant publicist for her mom's favorite author.

Julia types her name and number and hands the phone back to

London. A few seconds later, her own phone buzzes with a text: *Let's hang out.*

The opening date for the nonexistent Little Free Library approaches like a bullet train, and Fry's number is a 25. *I'm busy*, Julia texts back.

Across the table, there's a click as London slaps down her twinkly phone. "Doing what?" she hisses. "Homework? I've seen your grades. You don't *do* homework."

"It's not that…"

Another long blink. "Tell me."

Julia considers London. Her bright hair and perfect clothes are light years away from Julia's world of old trucks and used books. "I have to work on stuff," she whispers.

"Stuff," London repeats. "What stuff, exactly? I think you're full of shit."

Cold anger prickles in Julia's veins, and the chemistry room seems to disappear. There's no red number, no teacher, no other students. It all narrows down to London's annoyance, plainly obvious in the girl's beautiful face. "Look, I worked my ass off to get funds for a Little Free Library. A – a bookshelf, shaped like a house." Next to her, Bash moves suddenly and makes the chair squeak on the floor. Julia ignores it, her words tumbling over themselves, maybe because London actually seems to be paying attention. "I put it up in the park, and some asshole rammed it with a car last week. And whoever it was took off like it didn't matter after they destroyed everything I worked to create…"

London interrupts. "Bash. What's the hell's wrong with you?"

Intent on her complaints, Julia has forgotten all about the dark, moody boy across the table. She starts to apologize, but he cuts her off. "What did you just say?" His voice is nearly a whisper.

"Some idiot hit a project she spent a lot of time on. That's what I got out of it, anyway." London seems to give up on Julia and turns her attention back to her phone.

In front of the class, Mr. Fry puts up notes about the noble gases. He's a good teacher, Julia thinks. Wears a tie, looks like a stock image for the

'Dedicated Professional' tag. Fry looks up, startled, as Bash pushes back his chair with a loud screech and strides away from their table.

"I have to…" He doesn't finish his sentence, just strides to the back of the room. The classroom door opens and closes, and his footsteps die out in the hall.

Mr. Fry clears his throat. "All right, don't worry about the student who just broke a major school rule. Eyes up here."

"For fuck's sake, everyone's on drugs today." London rolls her eyes at the ceiling and plops her phone into an enormous lavender leather purse.

Julia remembers the embrace between Bash and London outside Isaac's party. Is there something between them? She wants to ask for details, but Mr. Fry begins a long monologue on the inert nature of argon.

When she looks up from her notes, London has also disappeared. Julia's all alone at the lab table.

• • •

Cursing his bad luck, Bash stomps through knots of students and teachers. He remembers the shock of impact on the Dart when he jumped the curb in the park. At the time he'd been too worried about the bottles under his passenger seat.

Did he hit something else after his wheel well scraped concrete? At the time he'd been intent on getting his ass out of the park. The following morning Bash found a dent in the right bumper – he remembers it clearly, since that had been the day of Isaac's party. He's already fixed it, using his grandfather's tools.

But by some weird twist in space, time, and fate, his car has taken out a Little Free Library, whatever that is. Bash can still hear the despair in Julia's voice, the way her words erupted as though she couldn't keep her anger inside any longer.

He can understand the feeling.

Julia. She's quiet. Pretty. Gets bad grades. He's seen the flush on her neck when the teacher hands her a quiz paper with angry red notes on the margin. Never caught Bash looking at her.

Probably because she's been intent on a horizon event, apparently, which he and the Dart destroyed. The honorable thing to do is to walk back and confess he was the one behind the wheel. Maybe there's a way to put things right, even now.

"Hey!" London's voice. Her shoes scuff the dirty school tiles and the concrete steps heading down to the school parking lot. Long fingers wrap around his bicep, and she tugs on his arm. "What the hell? Where are you going?"

Bash avoids the scalpel of her blue stare, tells her it's nothing. "I think Nehi might need me," he lies. "Had to get out of there."

She tows determinedly behind him, a mermaid on a boat line. "Don't give me your line of bullshit. What happened in Fry's class?" London tugs his shirt. "I *know* you. What Julia said back there made you weird. Why? Do I need to kick her ass?"

Bash gets his sleeve out of London's fist and heads to the Dart. She stays there and yells his name a few times. He knows she'll stand in the parking lot and watch him drive away, but he refuses to look back.

Do murderers really return to the scene of the crime? Bash has always thought such a thing would be a stupid move, a way of begging to get caught. But now he wants to drive back to Blue Anchor Park and check out the crash site.

It's not as though he really hurt anyone. No, the Dart's bumper just took out an object called a Little Free Library. Bash still has no idea what the phrase means.

It's surrender, a slow slide into a cold lake, to turn out of the parking lot and head towards the park. Bash navigates the map of roads mindlessly. Alcohol aids in the release of dopamine, he tells himself, the pleasure drug created by the human brain, while limiting the actions of a neurotransmitter called glutamate. The drinker becomes thoughtless and happy – or at least less sad for a while.

The Dart turns as if it drives itself. Bash watches the soccer fields and tennis courts stream past his window. Already there are a few players on the grass, tiny athletes with parents in tow. One woman yells at a boy wearing shin guards, her face red with anger. Bash hears her muffled shouts about lost opportunities and keeping your eyes on the prize.

The arterial street becomes a vein, a capillary, and the Dart coughs to a stop among an anonymous group of trees with gray humps of tombstones just visible through the woods. It's peaceful there, far away from the soccer fields.

Julia picked a nice place, he thinks.

But of course, he can't just sit there. Bash needs to remove any trace of his presence and get the hell out, back to Nehi and the barn.

He gets out and turns around, scanning the place where he destroyed Julia's thing, whatever it was. The curb is scarred with the distinctive cream paint of his 1970 Dodge. Although Bash feels that clue alone screams his guilt, in truth no one would probably recognize that retro color unless they looked for it. It could be… a spilled chai latte, or an extra-large bird poop. Probably there are lots of eagles and vultures in state parks.

Shaking his head at his own inanity, Bash turns back to his car. He pops the trunk and searches through the toolbox stashed there just in case.

There're a few squares of sandpaper under a jumble of screwdrivers and drill bits. The grade is rough, strong enough to erase the last of the evidence.

Bash looks around to make sure he's alone before squatting beside the pavement to sand off the paint. His fingers are scarred from dozens of his own projects, making things from wood the way his grandfather taught him when the old man was still alive.

Only the faraway traffic and the soccer players' voices filter through the trees to him. Maybe one is that angry mom shouting at her kid, or maybe the players are on the field and what Bash hears is joy.

It would be nice to listen to happiness, even if it's not his.

The paint is ground into the curb, and he has to wrap the sandpaper around a block to work the evidence out. The color's called Alpine White.

He saw the name in an old automobile pamphlet his grandfather had in their barn, carefully saved from when the old man bought the car.

When Bash finishes, the curb is stripped of Alpine White. He backs up, tilts his head on one side, and considers his work. The block goes back into the toolbox inside the trunk, and out of habit, he folds the sandpaper into careful quarters before stuffing it into his right back pocket.

There's another object in the back, just above the right rear wheel well. It clinks against the car's spare metal interior and sloshes when Bash picks it up.

He's almost forgotten it was there. The cap unscrews easily to release its genie, the instant and overwhelming odor of cheap tequila.

• • •

Julia can't afford a full tank, but ten bucks' worth of gas will get her through the next couple of days. As she waits under the Buy the Way awning, Julia plays with the radio, which is playing songs she's heard a thousand times before. Even the edgy Princeton college station has been preempted by a baseball game.

The jangle of her phone cuts into the crack of a bat and cheers from the college crowd. "Julia?" someone says.

She doesn't recognize the male voice or the number on her screen. "Who is this?"

"It's Isaac. Is it – is it okay that I called you?"

The attendant appears at her window, looking expectant, and she balances the phone between one ear and her shoulder. "Hang on. Let me just take care of this." She pays, drives away from the pump, and pulls into an empty space to talk. "Sorry. How did you get my number? You were out of it at your party, to be honest."

"That's one way to put it, although I wasn't completely totaled. Anyway, there's nothing on Netflix and I'm bored. Want to meet for coffee?"

"Well. I. Homework." She doesn't feel the need to see Isaac again. For one thing, filling her tank has left her without spare cash for overpriced caffeine. Plus, Julia has to do some serious thinking about the Little Free Library project if it's going to happen at all.

"I know we just met, but Tiffany gave me a huge Starbucks gift card and I'll never drink it all. Just meet me there and you can work on math *and* get jittery on too much caffeine."

Isaac's reasons make Julia laugh for the first time in days. Plus, she has the suspicion he'll go on and on until she gives in.

• • •

The overloaded confection in front of Isaac is a cloud of caramel and chocolate shavings, making Julia's teeth hurt just from looking at it. "You're the sad girl," Isaac declares as he spoons up some of the whipped cream. "It's how I think of you."

Julia nearly spills her cup. "Excuse me?"

"I don't mean sad like pathetic. But you have this look of disappointment, like something's gone wrong recently."

"I'm not…" She sighs and tries again. "Okay. I worked really hard on a thing and it was destroyed. I guess it made me – well, pissed. Not sad."

"Ooh." He scooches forward on the plastic seat and clasps both hands around his Frappuccino. Isaac's fingers are long and tapered, his most beautiful feature. "This doesn't sound like the usual coffee shop conversation. Tell me *everything*."

Ghost raises her eyebrows in surprise, and Julia swallows a scalding mouthful before answering. "A person I knew, someone really important, liked a book by a famous author, Hillman Minx. Ever heard of him?" Isaac just shrugs. "Okay, he's Goodreads-famous. We're not talking Neil Gaiman, but he's big in certain circles. Anyway, I got him to agree to come and do an appearance right here in Blue Anchor, but now it's not going to happen."

Once she's launched into the story she feels like a racer who has sprinted out of the blocks. It's impossible to stop. For the second time that day Julia explains what happened to the Little Library box in the park. In between details she notices that Isaac is a good audience, listening closely and humming with attention at intervals.

"You know, I could replace the box you lost," Isaac offers.

Her straw slurps in the empty cup, and Julia pushes away her ice coffee. "No way. Those things cost lots of money."

"It would help us both out. Seriously. Do you know how deliriously happy my mom would be if I spent her cash on a cool charity thing instead of video games or alcohol?"

"Isaac, I can't let you just shell out hundreds of dollars for a free-standing library bookshelf. We hardly know each other."

"'We hardly know each other,'" he mocks. "You're so cool and prim, like a secretary from an old movie, those black and white ones they show at 3 am when everyone's asleep." Isaac shifts his chair closer. "How do you buy one anyway, just order one of those boxes over the Internet? You got an iPad or laptop or something?"

She stifles a hoot of laughter. "Nope, definitely no iPad."

He pulls out his phone instead and starts swiping at it. Intent on the screen, he gets up and switches his seat to the chair next to hers. As they stare at the options popping up on Google, Isaac's voice gets high and excited over the Little Free Library shopping site options: a British phone booth, a farmhouse, a two-story Colonial. "I'm gonna buy you the most expensive one," he concludes.

"Isaac, cut it out!" Julia can't help laughing again at his determination.

Intent on pulling out a credit card from a black leather wallet, Isaac sees something on the screen and wilts. "When did you say you need this box?"

"Four weeks. Hillman Minx has a trip lined up after our opening, so I have to make it happen by then."

"These are all back-ordered," Isaac groans. "Can't get one for the next few months."

That figures. "Of course." Julia falls back against the seat, winded by her disappointment. "Did you ever feel like you were cursed?"

Isaac looks at her sideways. "I'm as bummed as you are." He grits his teeth, squeezes his eyes shut, and rams his head suddenly on the table. The bang startles the barista, who jumps and glares at their table.

"There's no need for that. Jesus, I slaved for months to buy the thing, and you don't see me slamming my face into furniture." Julia shoves back her chair with a loud squeal, ready to leave.

He reaches out with both arms and makes grabby motions with his hands. "Julia. Don't. I know I'm a fuck-up, but don't leave me. Please? Can't we go to your house and do homework?"

"You mean, come to my house and watch me do homework while you play games on your phone?" She feels one corner of her lips twist into a skeptical knot.

Isaac's grin, under his spiked hair, is unrepentant. "Well, yeah."

"You have to be polite to my dad." Julia feels like she's just adopted an unwanted puppy.

"Politeness is my specialty," Isaac insists.

• • •

Despite all of his showy and rebellious varnish, Isaac calls Julia's dad Mr. Cameron and shakes hands. There's soup on the stove, as usual, and he sniffs enquiringly.

"Potato," Julia's dad says. "Want to stay for dinner?"

"Sure." Isaac's smile is lazy. "Got any video games?"

Dad makes it clear homework comes first and it's going to get done in the family room instead of a bedroom. As Julia hands Isaac a glass of tap water and gets out her heavy chemistry book, her father hovers in the edge of her vision like a moth, a blowing curtain, a shadow.

She knows his sounds by heart. A clunk of the special dinner tray on their old kitchen Formica is followed by the soft lap of soup into her mom's green porcelain bowl and the clatter of a spoon. These are followed by hesitant footsteps as her dad carries a meal no one will eat to a room where nobody lives.

"Don't judge. It keeps him alive," Ghost whispers into Julia's hair. "He doesn't have anything else right now."

Isaac, who has proved to be sharp-eyed and intelligent when he's not wasted, watches the entire performance, and Julia pushes his elbow to distract him from the dinner tray performance. "You were a perfect gentleman with my dad," she adds.

"Surprised?"

"Sure. But – chem homework." She opens the chemistry textbook to the compounds section.

"Ugh. Tell me about Bash," Isaac probes. "How'd you two meet?"

Julia looks up from the rings of H's and O's combining in incomprehensible patterns. It's a lot more fun to talk about his party. "Bash? Why are you – well, I met him in school, I guess. But I know London better."

"London is a bright spot in this backwards New Jersey town. I love her clothes! Nobody has such fashion sense. In fact, we should go shopping together sometime, the three of us." Isaac's light eyes flick over Julia's old shirt and jeans.

Julia shrugs and attempts to create a chain of atomic compounds as he talks, but the atomic numbers just don't add up. Her mom once said it was a logic problem. "If you find the right sequence it'll all fit together," Ghost reminds her, "one atom at a time."

"I should finish this," she says in the middle of Isaac's rambling.

"Can I see?" He cranes his neck to peer at her page of problems. "Ew, those equation thingies. Stuff like that was why I gave up on school."

"Right about now I don't blame you. But do you mean you're not going to school at all? No classes? What do you do all day?" Julia pursues.

"You're looking at it. Persuade Tiffany and Mark to go out so I can throw more parties. Beg Tiffany for money. Go buy coffee. Play games."

She slumps back on the couch, winded by the gray existence he describes. "Don't you get bored?"

"All the time."

Her diner job comes to mind. "If you want I could get you…"

Isaac's pale eyes blaze suddenly. "A girlfriend? That's what you're going to say, right? I don't *want* a girlfriend! Jesus, when will people stop trying to make me be 'normal'?" He spits the last word with venomous anger.

Julia's pen and book slide sideways on her lap as she leans forward to explain. "That's not what I was going to say at all. In fact, I was going to offer you a job. It's nothing fancy, just bussing tables at the diner where I work, but at least it'll get you out of the house."

"Oh." Isaac raises one pale eyebrow and wilts back into his seat. "Sorry."

"Everyone's trying to hook you up, huh?"

He slides closer. "You have no idea. Tiffany always produces these girls for me, although now she's moved on to boys as well. I guess… I just wish someone could see me for what I really am."

"Which is what, exactly?" Julia clears her throat. "If you feel like telling me, I mean."

"I just don't…" Isaac waves one hand in the air. "I don't touch people other than hugs or quick kisses. I like going out, but at the end the person I'm with always expects something physical, and I'm just not into it."

"You like being friends, just not the romance part?" Julia wants to understand. He's unusually fervent as he speaks about his internal condition.

"No, that's not it at all. I *love* romance, flirting, having someone dress up for me, dressing up for them as well. But I might be asexual." He tilts his head and leans on one cheek. "It's, you know. Tough. I tried so many times, had sex with a few girls and one guy. It was like, I don't know, licking a penny. I didn't get anything out of it except a bad taste in my mouth." For once his ironic humor disappears, and she realizes that Isaac has hidden layers under that flimsy exterior. "No, that's not what I mean to say. I actually had to… get out of my head while it was happening, like I escaped into a secret place."

She nods. "Disassociation."

"Yes! Disassociation. That's the word I was looking for."

Julia bites her bottom lip. "Hey. Being ace is becoming pretty mainstream. You could probably find a bunch of people who feel the same way online – I mean to talk to, not to date."

His fingers twist into his spiky haircut. "You think I haven't tried that? There's support out there, but it doesn't make it easier. Everyone I meet wants to hook up. I can see it right from the start, their endgame, except for me the game is the end."

"Did you always know?" Julia shakes her head. "Sorry. Don't answer if it makes you uncomfortable."

Isaac slurps some tap water from his glass. "I thought was normal to never think about sex. Other people talked about it, but I never did."

"Normal," Julia repeats. "Why worry about what's normal? As far as I'm concerned, you are normal, not that it really matters what I think."

His eyes widen. "Yeah?"

"Yeah. Except for your 80's fashion sense, and there's nothing to be done there." He laughs, and Julia doodles a quick sideways 8 on the margin of her chemistry notes. "You want to come to the diner tomorrow during my shift and put in an application?"

He studies her before gusting a long breath. "I guess. Tiffany would probably do back flips with joy if I got a job."

"You'll lug dirty dishes around a diner filled with truckers, not taste champagne or polish tiaras."

It earns her another quick laugh. "Want to hang out this weekend? No, forget I ever asked. Sorry."

One corner of Julia's mouth curls up. "Maybe one day we can go to the park to look for clues to my Little Free Library mystery."

"Mystery? I love mysteries." Immediately Isaac launches into a planned shopping list of amateur detective gear like fingerprint kits and magnifying glasses. After he gets excited and nearly knocks over his glass of water, Julia regrets bringing it up.

With a sense of relief, she abandons the chemistry homework. They go to the kitchen and eat potato soup out of mugs around the scarred kitchen table while Julia's dad hovers in the background. Apparently

CHAPTER 2.

assured that Isaac as a normal guy who isn't a rapist, Tom retreats to the living room and his computer and finally leaves them alone.

Isaac finishes his fifth cup of soup and regards Julia, his chin propped on one fist. "Bet you have better dinners at home," she blurts. "All we ever eat is soup."

"Are you kidding? Meals usually come in plastic clamshell containers Tiffany brings home from an expensive Italian deli." Isaac's bright face folds into a frown.

The sudden glower makes Julia think about Bash and compare him to Isaac. One's solid and solitary, the other brittle and outgoing. One's dark and one is bright.

The real question is how she ever got so involved.

CHAPTER 3.

After finishing a long list of chores, Bash hides out in the barn where his grandfather used to keep chickens, ducks, even a few goats. Shadow, a sulky old Shetland rescue pony from a circus, lived in one stall and bit anyone who came near. Nehi was the only one who could get close, so she always had to feed the horse.

He remembers finding the pony one morning, limp and laid out in his stall, so quiet it hurt Bash's chest, and he shouted the pony's name. His voice was still changing at the time, and the name came out all wrong like a rusty squeal: "Shadow! Shadow!"

The pony lumbered to its feet, crazy and pissed-off as ever, and tried to charge. It ended up pinning him in the stall door before Nehi rescued him, shaking with pent-up laughter.

He grins at the memory and strides to the back of the barn where he's stashed an old folding chair. It screeches as he slumps into it.

His homework is organized inside his pants pockets, as usual. Bash pulls out wedges of handouts and notes written in his block capitals, and stacks them on the table's scratched surface. History in one pile, American Lit in another. He pushes the piles into perfect alignment with fingertips roughened from the sandpaper he used to remove all the Alpine White paint on the pavement. One edge sticks out, and Bash refolds the paper until it's squared-off like the other. Chemistry is the main assignment, a write-up of what the students are required to include in their papers.

After his royal screw-up in Fry's class, he'll have to get an A to compensate. And as for what he did in the park...

Bash looks at the neat piles of notes and assignments. *What the hell is wrong with me?* The thought bullets through axons and neurons, at least 100 billion of them inside his head. He knows there's a paper missing, but he's so tired he can't remember what it is. At least leaving school early has given him a few minutes of silence, but soon it will be time to do his main task: that sick little ritual.

There's enough time to do math homework first, maybe some English as well. Chemistry will have to wait until after dinner so he can concentrate his hardest. It's just like putting together a wood project after all, the search for a pattern before he lines up the words or numbers into perfect order, and as usual he forgets the time.

When he realizes how late it is, Bash curses. He shoves all the paper squares into his left pocket and stands up, letting the chair falls backwards into an old pile of straw. His boots are loud on the ancient oak slats, laid over mud when the barn was built, as he strides outside.

A slice of the farmhouse is visible through the door. It never fails to give him a cold chill when he sees a black shape at Nehi's window.

Blood-orange sunlight glints off the glass. From where Bash stands, Nehi moves like a soybean cyst nematode under a microscope.

Does Nehi see me here in the barn? Is she waving? Does she need help? Is she yelling for someone to get the hell upstairs?

No way to tell.

The land between the house and barn is covered with long wild grass and unchecked flowering weeds. A track leads from the barn through the pines behind the property, pointing northward like an arrow or a scar.

Bash closes his eyes for a moment. As much as he hates himself, he has to do it.

It's like walking on the moon. The house wavers on his right, the barn on the left. Bash follows the track through waist-high grass.

"I don't want to," he says out loud. The wildflowers swallow his words.

Helplessly, Bash continues up to the pines. He sees where the needles are scuffed into piles, because he knows exactly what to look for. No one else would recognize the track.

His prize is under a downed holly tree. Bash curses as he thrusts one arm between the sharp, pointed leaves. They scratch him with witchy fingernails as he withdraws the hidden prize from a triangle of roots:

A bottle of rye whiskey.

• • •

Later, Bash stumbles out of the barn and up to the house. Two lights are on, luminous rectangles in the dark. One is from the kitchen, where he nearly knocks over a glass near the sink.

The other is upstairs.

Bash goes to the upper floor, stepping on the outside of the stair treads so Nehi won't hear him and wake up. The second light is inside her room, although it can't be seen from the hall.

He stops beside Nehi's door. It's closed on the outside with a simple hatch repurposed from the barn after their last goat was sold off to pay some bills. The hatch flap is secured by an old combination lock from Bash's middle school gym class.

The knob twirls in his hand and clicks, and Bash opens the door to look inside. The occupant seems to be asleep on the bed. Nehi lies as still as Shadow once did, that long-ago morning in the pony stall, and for a moment his heart stops.

No. She's still alive. In the warm lamplight, the woman's sheet lifts and falls, a tiny motion caused by her breath.

Bash holds his breath and shuts off the light. Nehi doesn't make a sound. He doesn't exhale until he's out in the hall once more, the hatch on her door secured by his lock.

What about Julia, the girl from Chemistry class? What would she say if she could see him now?

I couldn't help it, Bash imagines telling her. *I don't want to be like this.*

Maybe Julia would turn away in disgust or call the cops. No, telling her anything about himself is out. He can't risk it.

The little pile of papers gets lined up onto the dresser. Bash pitches onto the bed, still in jeans, t-shirt, and boots. He simply doesn't have the energy to get undressed.

"I'm sorry," he whispers again to the girl who isn't there. In his imagination, Julia stands next to the bed, slim and upright in his room, one eyebrow raised like an accusatory question-mark.

"Don't worry," Bash slurs. "Somehow, I'll fix it."

CHAPTER 4.

Julia gets a D+ on the chemistry test. She can't see Bash's grade, although she can see his reaction. He raises one eyebrow and lowers both corners of his mouth before folding the test into a neat square.

She does her best to concentrate on class, even though she's tired from her shift at the diner. When she finally turns 18 she'll be able to work longer hours. It'll mean late nights but more money when the life insurance checks stop.

Her eyelids slide shut and the room shifts sideways. Julia falls into a dream of bookshelves and empty beds, of soup pots and the impossible college goal.

A folded square pushed into the crook of her arm startles her, and she shifts back to the reality of class as she unfolds the note. Written on the top line are neat capitals: WHAT IS A LITTLE FREE LIBRARY?

Bash is looking at her intently, his dark eyes expectant. Julia looks back down at the paper he's passed her, makes a decision, and scrawls out a quick answer. *It's a small, public place for people to get books when they want to read,* she explains. *The LFL organization has built them worldwide.*

Mr. Fry heads their way, looking over the shoulders of students working on the day's project in a grumpy silence. Unable to think of anything else to add, Julia waits until the teacher stalks back to the board before sliding the paper back to Bash.

His face is expressionless as he reads. Fry clicks past several bullet points about the internal astronomy of atoms on the screen before Bash's note nudges against the sensitive skin of Julia's inner arm.

SOUNDS BOGUS, Bash has written. SOMEONE WILL RIP IT OFF.

Julia scribbles a long explanation of what happened to the first box – how she washed cars and sold brownies. How she spent hours picking out the perfect box with the money. How she took it to the park, how a car appeared out of nowhere and reduced it to a pile of splinters in a hit and run.

When Julia hands over the note and shakes away the memory, Bash reads her scrawl with his usual frown before printing a response.

SO YOU'RE SAYING IT'S GONE.

Yeah, she writes. *Gone.*

Fry picks up a dry-erase marker and changes the circled number on the board to 24. The time to write the chemistry paper is ticking away, and Julia has no idea what to do for the assignment. If she doesn't come up with something soon, she'll fail the class.

Another pause. When the note comes back, five letters are written at the bottom.

SORRY.

In the adjacent chair, London raises one eyebrow, opens her mouth, and then closes it again. Obviously, she's figured out that actual notes are getting passed under her nose.

Bash reaches out and pulls the creased paper on Julia's notebook back to his desk before she can respond. When he returns it, there's a question spelled out in his firm capitals: LOCKER NUMBER? PS – NOT A CREEPER.

Julia feels her lips twitch up. Bash's the last person she would pick for being a creeper. In fact, she's never met anyone so internal, so stern, and so secretive. She doesn't know him, but his 'Back off' vibe is strong.

He's only asking for her locker, not her phone or social security number. Julia blows out a long breath, scrawls C414, and hands back the paper.

It seems their silent conversation is over.

After scribbling down Fry's assignment, Julia leaves the class and makes it to her locker where she rests her hot forehead against cool metal. Alone in a stream of students she blinks and wonders what the hell she's going to do with her growing host of problems.

"Why's this library thing so important?"

The abrupt question makes her stand up so suddenly she bangs her head against the top of her locker. Julia smothers a yelp and frowns at Bash. "Thought you said you weren't a creeper."

"I'm not. But I want to know why you're so stuck on the idea of a Barbie's Dreamhouse filled with books."

She's tired and her truck is going to run out of gas, and if things don't turn around soon Julia won't even make it into community college. Plus, there's her dad at home, probably in the kitchen with a pot on the stove. He could be ladling soup into another bowl right now, prepping a tray for the empty bed, lying to himself about the person who is gone.

Julia slams her locker shut, drops her backpack, and faces him. Bash is a few inches taller, so she's forced to tilt up her chin. "I built it to remember someone important," she says. "A memorial, I guess you could say. But the whole thing's fucked, like I told you in that note. I guess you overheard the other day when I was telling London about this whole sorry situation." She feels like she's talking too much. "Anyway, I have to…"

"I build things," Bash says. "Out of wood. My grandfather turned the tack-room in our barn into a workspace."

It's a proclamation out of nowhere. "Oh," Julia replies after a second. "Good for you, and for him. Well, um, I've got to go home."

"You're leaving?"

"Yeah." Julia picks up her books and digs for the keys to her truck. He's got his arms folded, head tilted back so he can look down his nose at her. The long curls around the dark skin of his neck are like licks of black paint. There's no phone in his hand, and he doesn't carry a backpack.

"You keep all your stuff in your pockets?" she demands.

Bash's grumpy eyebrows knit themselves even closer. "Why?"

"Just wondering what happens when you do your wash. Did you ever send all your notes and assignments through the laundry?"

It earns her the fractional glimmer, a tiny deepening of the lines at the corners of his mouth. He doesn't look amused, merely less annoyed for a second. "Once," he answers.

Julia feels her lips tremble as she tries not to laugh. "Then you have to transfer everything over when you wear new pants? And I thought switching purses was bad."

"It's all highly organized," he insists. "Right brain stuff in right rear pocket – English goes there, obviously." A square hand taps one butt cheek to illustrate. "Math and science on the left side. Electives in the front."

"How about that little coin pocket no one ever uses?"

He laughs, a short and surprised sound. "Saving it for something special. Uh, you have a lot of hair."

"Carrot soup," Julia blurts.

"What?"

"My hair's the color of carrot soup." Figuring she's embarrassed herself enough, Julia picks up her books and stalks out to the school parking lot.

• • •

Aggie's Diner shimmers with warmth from the steam table and the hissing grill. Aggie herself still uses classic diner lingo, shouting "Adam and Eve on a raft and wreck 'em," to Ben, the cook. Her hair is even redder than Julia's ringlets: a rich scarlet Aggie calls Clairol #29. She was married to Ben years ago. After the divorce, they continued to yell at each other across the diner about orders of 'elephant dandruff' and 'pigs between the sheets' interspersed with 'Aggie, you are such a mean bitch.'

"Clean the kitchen, y'ole bastard." Aggie yells her code for hash as Julia ties on her red apron. Ben bends over the stained grill, not deigning to look up as he gives Aggie the finger. A row of gloomy truckers hunch over their plates with cups of coffee at their elbows. More customers are lined up by the cash register, waiting for tables or one of the booths.

The diner is popular, since Ben insists on cooking with nothing but real butter and eggs. It's been featured on Road Show and in a local column called Cheap 'n' Tasty.

Julia stashes her backpack behind the washing machine, grabs a tray, and zeroes in on the tables most in need of bussing. Reenie, the other waitress, gives her a quick "Hey, honey," before flipping out an order pad and reciting the specials to a family in the corner booth.

A few kids squabble over who's going to use the family's iPad. Their parents slump in the opposite seat, the mother's face lined with bad makeup and exhaustion.

Julia's arms tire quickly, but she's used to physical labor. The plastic dish bins get filled with bowls, forks, and steel milkshake cups before she hauls them to the dishwasher, reflecting that the quick pace keeps Julia from worrying about grades and the Little Free Library. It's almost a relief to concentrate on plates painted with egg yolk and ketchup instead of all she's lost.

She hands out crayons to kids and mops up spilt Coke as the patrons swim in and out of her vision. The diner is like a brightly lit fish tank, an oasis of noise and food along the darkening stretch of Route 73.

Aggie taps her on the shoulder and jerks her head in the direction of the bar. "Clean up in Aisle Ben."

"Again? Okay." Julia dumps the truckers' coffee cups, rinses them, and fills the partitioned sink stack. One guy has left his number scrawled on a napkin, and she holds it up to make Aggie laugh.

"Hey Ben! Looks like I'm leaving you." Aggie hollers as she waves the flimsy square with smeared digits written in blobby ink. "Again."

"Nah, that trucker's *my* future ex-husband," Reenie argues.

"Give it here." Ben stalks out, grabs the napkin, and balls it up.

"Maybe the guy left it for him," Reenie hisses in a stage whisper, making Aggie cough with laughter.

Julia's in the middle of scrubbing dried mustard off a booth seat when Isaac slips into the diner, an unrepentant ghost dressed in tight black jeans and a red jacket. He grins at her as she beckons him over and shakes her head exaggeratedly at his outfit with a loud Tut Tut. "You're applying for a diner job, not auditioning for a hipster musical," she adds.

"Aw, c'mon, Jule. You know you love me." He slides into a bar seat, spins back and forth experimentally, and orders coffee. "Mind if I call you Jule?"

"Actually, I kinda do." Julia gets him his coffee. "Are you still excited for the job?"

"Tiffany smiled when I told her I was going for it. Actually smiled. I didn't know she could after all her Botox injections." Isaac blows on his cup and stirs in far too much sugar.

"Ha ha." Julia shifts her bucket of dishes to one hip. "Aggie, okay if my friend fills out an application for a bussing job?"

"Sure." Aggie's shrewd brown eyes take in Isaac's pale, spiked hair and earlobe plug. "This your boyfriend? Reenie, Julia's got a boyfriend!"

"She could do better," Reenie sniffs.

Julia tries to argue he's not her boyfriend, but Isaac has a huge grin on his face, eyes alight with interest. "Good evening," he proclaims. "Do either of you ladies have a pen?" *What a diva,* Julia thinks. He's a beautiful, attention-starved swan.

Reenie hands him a ballpoint, and Aggie gives him the back of a placemat to write his contact information. "Put down your experience, too," she tells him.

"That'll be easy," Isaac blurts. "I don't have any."

"Sure you do," Julia interrupts. "Event organizer."

"Oh, riiight. Event organizer." Isaac winks at her and scribbles it down.

Aggie gives him another hard glance. "Start you on a shift a week," she declares. "One mistake and you're out."

"Really?" Julia can tell Isaac's delighted. He throws Aggie an air-kiss, and she tells him to get lost before marrying two ketchup bottles and hiding her grin. "This is awesome, Jule, seriously."

She can't help getting sucked in by his childish delight over a handful of diner shifts that don't even amount to a real job yet. "Drink your sugar, Ize," she says.

"Ize? Oh." He winks and pretends to shoot her with one finger raised from his cup. "Very clever."

"I have my moments." It's easy to talk to Isaac, almost peaceful.

"What's the story with your dad?"

Julia sets down the dirty dishes with a clatter. "Nothing. What do you mean? I mean, he's in-between jobs if that's what you're saying, and…"

"And what?" A dark shape fits itself into the seat next to Isaac. Bash, of all people. He glares at Julia, and she blinks at him.

"Uh. Hi." She stands up so suddenly she nearly clocks Reenie, who's passing with a load of burgers and fries on a tray. "I didn't expect... How did you – did you just get here?"

Isaac's smile returns, a slumped parenthesis of mischief and glee. "Hi, Bash," he murmurs into his coffee cup.

Bash ignores him and slits his eyes at Julia. "You never answered my question," he says.

"You know, I might be an asexual freeloader with zero game, but I'm pretty sure that's not how it's done." Isaac finishes his coffee with one final, annoying slurp.

"Wasn't talking to you." Bash keeps his black gaze on Julia's face.

Reenie passes with an order of pie, whispering something about more boyfriends than she can handle and maybe Julia could share.

"You know what? I'm choking on the testosterone right about now, and it's my break. Reenie, get them both more coffee and put it on my tab." Julia slaps her rag over one shoulder, spins on one sneakered heel, and heads to the back where Ben and Aggie are bickering as usual. They keep at it as Julia gets a scarred plastic glass, fills it with Ben's pitcher of iced tea.

"Julia's got two boyfriends and won't share," Reenie calls through the window. She hooks her slip on the order carousel and escapes before Julia can retort.

"Two of 'em? Oh Lord, you poor thing. One man was bad enough for me."

"I was a prince," Ben growls at Aggie's back. "A prince, you hear me?" He snitches a look at Julia and lowers his voice. "Need me to shove a fist in someone's face?"

Julia laughs and drinks more tea. "Tempting, but I'll take care of it myself."

Ben expertly flips six sizzling patties and douses them with his own secret spicy salt mixture, kept grill-side in a large tin shaker. "Hmm," he says. "Offer stands. You just let me know."

• • •

Julia drives home in a fog of exhaustion and worry. She doesn't see the slew of texts until she's in pj's and sitting up in bed within a circle of lamplight. Isaac has sent her a video of himself doing a crazed dance under a stop sign, holding a fedora.

In stark contrast, the other thread of messages is somber. It's straight to the point in Bash Language, which Julia thinks she's starting to understand. *Things on my mind,* he writes. *Can we meet up? My barn.* There's a ten-minute, thoughtful pause before he adds, *Lots of light there. Good place to work.*

"Someone's popular," Ghost cackles.

His name floats next to the 'incoming text' dots. Obviously, he's trying to explain himself. Julia takes pity on him and calls his number, figuring things will move faster if they have a conversation.

"I can't talk," Bash says as soon as he picks up. "Wait – I don't mean it like that. Just hold on one second."

Julia flaps back against the pillows and pleats her threadbare flat sheet as she waits. In the background she can't make out the words Bash says. Someone's talking back to him. Is it London?

"Hey."

"I didn't mean to bother you," Julia declares. "But it's quicker to set something up this way instead of texting back and forth all night." She can almost hear his rare smile, and she quickly adds, "Not that we'd text all night! I'm exaggerating. It's just easier... oh, never mind."

There's another pause, and she waits. The phone slips in her palm, and she steadies it with the other hand. "You know what would be even better? Face to face." Bash's words sound stretched and warm, as though he's actually smiling for once. "Doing anything tomorrow?"

"No." She doesn't have another shift until the weekend.

"Okay. You can follow me to my place after school, and I'll show you around the barn."

"Just follow you to your place," she says flatly.

"Not a creeper, I already made that clear." Bash clears his throat.

She decides not to argue. If she tells her dad and maybe Isaac as well first, it'll be safe. "Okay," Julia agrees. "Actually, while I have you on the phone – did you start your chemistry paper?"

A loud slap floats over the phone. "Got my notes filed right here, rear right pants pocket." She can picture his grumpy triumph and the crinkling sound the paper will make as he unfolds it to go over the notes.

Julia's voice lowers, and perhaps it's the exhaustion talking or maybe too much caffeine. "I'm not going to get a good grade," she mumbles. The confession is harsh in her lungs. She has no idea why she's telling Bash.

"No, you'll get an okay grade," he says immediately. "You know why? We'll go over Fry's write-up in my barn. I've got some a table and some chairs in one of the stalls. We could work there."

"Yeah?" Julia picks at the little sprouts of fluff on her old counterpane. "Maybe I should adopt your pants-pocket-filing-system. My version doesn't work out so well."

"It's a good system," he agrees. "Uh – by the way. I could build you a house."

"You're going to build me a house," Julia repeats. She waits, skin cooling in the chill of early spring. In the hallway she hears her dad's quiet sounds as he opens the laundry closet and starts up the washing machine.

"Maybe. One day." He's smiling again, Julia thinks. "In the meantime, I could make you another bookshelf like the one you lost. Shaped like a house. Which is what you want, right?"

Julia sucks in a breath and launches into a long, confused explanation of why she can't expect him to solve her Library problem. They're practically strangers. He's got homework. Plus, she doesn't need him. She'll figure it out on her own.

Bash interrupts, as if it's the quickest way to move out of her tangled argument. "Sounds like you're running out of time, so forget all those arguments. Bring a picture of what you want to build, since I'll need some kind of reference, and we can get started." His words speed up. "Of course, we'll end up riffing off it and doing what we want. Usually I start with one design and end up in a totally different place." He sucks in a breath and finishes, "You'll see what I mean once the piece is underway."

"You know what? It's late. I'm tired. And by the way, I haven't agreed to anything just yet." Julia wonders if her smile translates over bytes and packaged voice interface data, the way his does. "Good night."

She clicks the red button to end the call before turning off the light. Slowly the screen's glow fades, reserving power. Next to her, in the dark, Ghost tosses her head back and shakes with full-bodied laughter. "You're a natural-born flirt! No wonder you've got two boys ready to fight over you in the diner!"

"Not a flirt." Julia's too tired to argue. She can hear the thump of their old washing machines as her dad's laundry whirls into spin cycle, his way of clearing out the room where he sleeps. The weary house grumbles with popping nails and that one floorboard that always squeaks outside the empty bedroom.

But for once, things are different. Tomorrow will be different. For the first time in forever, Julia actually looks forward to it.

CHAPTER 5.

Bash brings her to a small tack-room off the stables in his barn. Julia follows and breathes in the scent of horses, wood shavings, and alfalfa. Even though the place is swept clean, dust galaxies swirl in the afternoon sun streaming in through the paned windows.

Julia glances into the old stalls and asks if Bash has animals in the stalls. His eyes flick sideways at her, the usual look of a suspicious guard determined to keep his life private. "One," he admits.

Julia doesn't press for details. "You really don't have to build me a house," she starts. "I mean, a bookshelf. Bookshelf-house."

He turns away but crooks his fingers, a come-on gesture. "At least come and look at my set-up before you make up your mind."

The tack-room is taken up with an old desk turned into a neatly organized workbench. Its surface is scarred, deep angles where some tool has bitten into the wood. A box of tiny drawers on the left is marked with handwritten labels: *sprig, tack, annular nails, lost head.* Some have numbers underneath, *12* or *16d.* "My grandfather made the bench," Bash comments when Julia peers at the labels. "He left me all his carpentry gear when he passed."

There's a metal toolbox on the right corner, rusted on the hinge. It squeaks when Bash opens it to show her several hammers, a selection of files, a few chisels.

"It's nice." Ugh, what a stupid comment. "I mean, I know less than nothing about tools and wood."

Bash just holds out one palm and asks if she brought a sample picture.

She holds his stare and produces a paper from the back pocket of her jeans. "Here." The image is printed out from online, the same model that got destroyed in the park. It's meant to look like an old schoolhouse with a slanted roof and windows on the sides.

"Won't hold too many books." He flicks the picture onto the bench.

"It's a *Little* Free Library," she points out.

"I get that, but…" With a sudden burst of energy, he sweeps dust and hay off the workbench with one arm, turns the picture over, and grabs a pencil from a Mason jar. "You could do something like this instead." Quick strokes outline a bigger house, one with two stories and more windows. "Fits more shelves inside, see? I'm guessing you want to have books available for all ages, so you could put the kids' stuff on the bottom. Easier to reach. Adult stuff goes on top."

Julia's eyes widen as his idea comes to life. It's good, more beautiful than even the thousand-dollar models she dreamed about before ordering the most basic design. "I only have a few weeks," she protests.

He sweeps his arm over his face as though he wipes away sweat along with her worries. "I'll graph it tonight and use the jigsaw to cut out the pieces. Lathe for those rounded columns. See? Should have everything ready next week to put together." Bash jabs at the bottom of the house with one thumb. "This isn't really load-bearing, and you never know what people will do with public property. Dovetail joints would make this really secure, but I don't know if we'll have enough time to get really fancy. Just have to do my best."

Although she's clueless about 'dovetail joints,' Bash's low, growly voice relaxes her. For one moment, Julia forgets her doubts. She leans against the bench and watches as he adds details to the sketch – a tiny porch, door trim, and a slot for the support post. She's so intent on the movement of his fingers she misses his question. "Sorry, what?"

"Does this look okay? I need your signed-off approval."

"Oh. I think it'll do." Julia can't help laughing at his sidelong glance. "It's better than what I had before – way better. I don't want to use up all your time, though."

The pencil gets clamped between his teeth, and he goes to the sliding barn door. Behind the knotted pine are shelves lined with more jars, huge mayonnaise containers filled with nails and screws. Screwdrivers hang from the back of the closet, organized by size. There are flat boxes labeled 'Drill Bits' and 'Sandpaper'. Bash reaches for a shallow drawer, opens it, and pulls out a roll of paper. "I can sketch it out on here," he says around the pencil. "Mark it out on Adobe later."

He uses the side of the workbench to tear off a broad swath of paper, takes down a bent metal ruler from nails set into the wall. "T-square. It's all about the angles. This is a simple project, but there's so much you can do with 360 degrees. There's a box in the closet behind us that holds drill bits and small parts like that. My grandfather made it. Go ahead, take a look." He waves at the wall behind them, and Julia realizes it's actually a sliding door built with U-shaped hanging hinges.

Julia steps over the rough concrete of the floor, pushes back the door on its bar, and finds the handmade box before carefully picking it up. Bash's grandfather used dark wood and   partitioned the interior with diamonds, each filled with various sizes of drill bits. A closer look shows the genius behind the partitions – they assemble as one complete unit, the strips weaving in a deceptively simple pattern. The maker would have had to measure each piece separately, certain they would come together at the end.

"Turn it around." Bash watches her. "See how the hinge is set right into the wood so there's no line? No one bothers to do that anymore – just screw on a hinge so it hangs out. Guess they figure no one looks at the back of a box."

He's right. When she brushes her fingertips over the brass hinge, she can't feel the separation between wood and metal. Ghost hooks her chin over Julia's shoulder, intent on the treasures inside the old barn. Julia slides her a side glance, and Ghost raises one finger to her lips.

"He's guy with secrets," Ghost breathes in Julia's ear.

Well, he's not the only one.

Julia closes the box and puts it back in the closet. When she rejoins Bash, his sketch has grown into a grid of different components. The sides, the floor, and a frame for the door are all sketched out in neat, competent lines. "Needs to be weather-stripped," Bash says, "but that's simple enough. And the door should have a closing mechanism so some loser doesn't leave it open in a rainstorm. I've got some strong magnets and a spring we can use."

A terrible thought hits her, and she opens her mouth, closes it. "Actually, we didn't talk about…"

"Wood can be weird," he interrupts. "The project has to stand up to rain and snow, obviously. Tar paper will take a lot of abuse, but the wood should be good stuff. Cedar's the obvious choice, although it can split when you're working with it. Treated wood is an option, I guess, but you never know when some kid's going to chew on it. But guess what? I have a ¾" panel of white oak."

Julia does some quick mental arithmetic. If she stops taking the truck to school she can pay him for all the supplies in a month or two, depending on how much white oak costs. "Bash," she starts.

"What?" Bash looks up from the drawing, his mouth tense with concentration.

Julia scratches her wrist. "Well, um. Money."

His upside-down smile seems to mean he's thinking. "Got some teak that came from a tree in Benin, at least that's what the dealer said. Picked it up really cheap at a lumber auction. I can sketch a little cupola, or use it for door trim."

"Um." Julia flounders. "Thing is, I might take a while to pay you back for all this. Better forget the teak and stick to the cheap stuff. You know?"

He puts down his pencil and leans on the table to frown at her. "What are you talking about?"

Julia jerks her thumb at the closet. "This wood has to be expensive, from what you told me – weather-resistant and junk. I spent everything I raised on the first box, so I'm going to have to owe you for a while, pay it off slow." Her voice tails off. His gaze skewers her.

"I wasn't going to charge you," he says.

"What? No. You can't just *give* me this stuff. Not to mention your time. Damn, I'm an idiot. Probably we should have talked about this before."

The peace of the barn spills out the late sunlight. In one of the far stables Julia hears something rustle. *Rats? God, please don't let it be rats.* "Tell you what." Bash picks up his pencil and stabs it in her direction. "I'll use that white birch and other stuff I've got hanging around the barn. You get an A on Fry's essay and we'll call it even."

"An A?" She shakes her head, still concentrating on the noises in the barn. "Why do you care about my grades?"

"Let's just say I don't like the expression on your face when you see those red marks all over your homework in class. Stay here and study with me, and we'll both ace that test. The essay you've got to do yourself, though."

The rustling intensifies, and Julia is startled when she hears a background *Wheek wheek wheek.* "What's in there?" she asks.

Bash's dark eyes crinkle into upside-down crescent moons. "It's my pig. Want to see?"

"A pig?"

He lays down his pencil and heads out of the tack room to the last stall in the barn. A large, open-topped cage runs along one side, and a small, orange guinea pig stands by an empty bowl, looking up expectantly. As soon as they get closer the wheeks get louder. "Meet Harley," he says.

"Harley?" Julia squats in the hay. Bash pulls a plastic bag of pellets out of a corner and pours food into the bowl. "Because he's a hog?"

"She. She's a hog."

"Hi, Harley." The guinea pig ignores them both and starts munching food with determined concentration. "What are those pellets made of?"

"Timothy hay. Although she really wants carrots. Right, piggy? And lettuce."

"I'll bring some for her next time." Julia realizes as soon as she says it she's established a connection, a future.

He rubs Harley's fur the wrong way as the guinea pig eats the pellets, making the animal vibrate with a distinct purr. "She likes that idea," he states. "Tomorrow?"

"I have to work tomorrow night," Julia says. "Saturday?"

"Saturday works. Tell you what, I've done all I can do for now until

I get those plans shaped up the way I want them. We could sit here and watch the pig chow while we study."

It might be the most original proposition she's ever had from a guy. As she waits for Bash to fetch their books she leans towards Harley to check out the guinea pig's solemn mouth and nostrils shaped like an elongated infinity symbol.

"You can hold her if you want." Bash dumps their stuff on the floor and folds himself into a pretzel next to the cage. "As long as you don't mind getting fur on your clothes and maybe some pig turds, although she's pretty clean."

"I think I can deal." Julia looks in her backpack. "Uh, do you know what we're supposed to study?"

Bash taps his left butt cheek, and his full lips curve into a secret smile. "I do. Got the notes folded up right here in my filing system."

CHAPTER 6.

London is hanging over Bash's desk when Julia comes into the room the next day. "And you haven't told her yet?" the girl asks.

His eyebrows shoot down into their customary V, and Julia catches his quick, piercing glint as he catches sight of her. Bash's sideways glance reminds her of Harley's permanently suspicious expression.

He hisses something under his breath and jerks away from the girl. Julia knows he's warning London to be quiet.

Mr. Fry hands out the papers, and the class settles into uncomfortable silence. Julia plops her backpack on the floor, settles into the hard chair, and pulls out a pen. She's ready for the test, more confident than she's been in a while for a class, but she can't ignore that overheard snippet of conversation. There's something going on between Bash and London, but it's not as though Julia can get upset over other people's untold secrets.

She forces her concentration onto the essay questions. The notes Bash took in his neat capitals have definitely helped, and for a moment Julia wonders if she might start using his pants-pocket system to help her grades.

As the kids write, Fry stalks around the desks. He's an angular stork of a man in black and white, insisting on suits even though most of the other teachers come to school in jeans.

London finishes early and hands in her test before starting in on the texts. As soon as the bell rings she asks, "Bash, are you actually going to make it to Isaac's tonight?"

"Isaac's not having a party," Julia says.

The cool up and down of London's perfectly mascara-coated lashes measure Julia and the papers spilling out of her backpack. "How the hell would *you* know?" London demands.

"I got him a job at the diner where I work. His first shift's tonight." Before either he or London can ask anything else, Julia yanks the zipper on her backpack shut and leaves.

She doesn't bother to stop at her locker.

• • •

Aggie's is packed on Friday nights from the moment Julia arrives for her shift until closing. "You're getting thrown right into the mix," she tells Isaac when he bounds into the back kitchen.

He wraps on one of the half-aprons around his hips and ties the ends into a bow. "I once worked in a sales office for two weeks. Sat in a desk for eight hours straight waiting for the phone rang. Lesson learned: busy is good."

"Well, time should fly tonight in that case." Julia picks up a bin and shows Isaac how to clear a table, stashing trash and dumping dishes. "The worst is when you get food artists, the ones who dump ketchup in the middle of leftover waffles and top the whole masterpiece with half a canister of sugar," she says.

"Hm. Food artist, is that what you call them? Just maybe I have been a food artist in the past. I guess I never thought about the person who cleared up later." He shudders as he picks up a mug by the handle, sloshing leftover hot chocolate into his bin. "Ew, ew, ew. Now I feel both gross and guilty."

They work steadily, replacing dirty plates with clean silverware and napkins. The line at the door inches in and grows longer for dinner. After a few hours of hauling plates, Aggie sends Julia and Isaac to the back for break and a quick sandwich each. When she's not looking, Ben sneaks them an extra order of fries. Isaac shoves them in his mouth, complaining about Tiffany's new quinoa obsession between bites. "It's like eating crunchy sand," he declares before smashing half a cheeseburger into his face. "And let's not even start on the chia pudding. She thinks I need to 'purge my system.'"

"My dad makes soup for dinner every single night. It's awesome to come here and eat food with a fork," Julia says. "And chew! Chewing is so underrated. By the way, I told London your party was canceled."

CHAPTER 6.

"Oh, I'll still have a party." Isaac's tone is sunny. "Just have to start at 2 am, though, like the clubs in Ibiza. You're coming, right?"

"So *not* coming."

Aggie's yelling for them to get back to work, and Julia dumps her platter in the sink, musing about the little library and Bash. One way or another she's going to confront him about his conversation with London. Bash may not be her boyfriend, but Julia refuses to get played.

"Why won't you come over and have a few drinks with me?" Isaac pursues her with eight mugs looped around his fingers. She has to admit he's a fast learner and a good worker for all his stagy, flippant mannerisms. "I thought we were friends."

She shakes her head, but he doesn't give up. Exasperated, Julia finally admits she might have found a way to rebuild her Little Free Library, and she needs sleep. Isaac is all instant attention, and he begs to come with her to see the project. "I want to see the house," he begs. It's what he calls it: 'the house.'

"No."

"Hey." Isaac puts the mugs into the crate and pulls her in for a quick hug before pleading in her ear, "Can we at least go to the park after work? To look for clues, like you said?"

"Not tonight."

• • •

The truck shudders as Julia pulls into the driveway and turns off the ignition. She sits in the cab for a minute, exhausted from her shift. The neighborhood has the aura of coming apart at the edges – there are milk cartons in the gutters, heaps of unused furniture on a neighbor's porch.

She heaves a sigh. Time to go in and face the silent house, the empty bedroom.

Julia pulls off her work shoes at the door and glares at the pile of books holding up the spot where her dad's armchair is missing a leg. He keeps saying he's going to fix it, but of course it never happens. By now the original piece is long gone, lost in a drawer or on a shelf somewhere.

Her dad sits in the chair, snoring softly with eyes closed and his chin propped up on one fist. The slant of his neck makes the lamplight shine on his graying hair and the bristles on his chin. Sleep shrinks him down, paring him to the bone.

She peers into the kitchen and sees the stockpot on the stove beside a cutting board littered with ends of celery and limp parsley. The mess makes her long for the neatly labeled boxes in Bash's barn.

When Julia's mother was still around the house was more contained. She wasn't one of those scrapbooking, project-driven parents, driving a slew of kids to travel soccer with a laptop in a duffel bag. But since her death, the house has shrunk. It winds its contents inwards like thread, encases itself in messy solitude.

Julia tells herself this is the existence she's used to. Her father once had a job in the city, but the loss of his wife has had the same shrinking effect. Always tall and broad-shouldered, lately he seems smaller. Julia can't remember the last time she's seen him laugh. They used to crack up together over stupid stuff: the next-door neighbor whose fussy chihuahua looked just like her, a puddle shaped like a butt. He used to throw his head back, slap his knee, kick out with one foot.

It's all gone, stolen by a drunk driver when Julia's mom was killed.

Her dad works from home during the day when he can find online data entry. In the afternoon he places an online order with a grocery delivery service. At night he makes soup.

She puts a hand on his shoulder. His eyes swivel like marbles under closed lids, negotiating the unknown landscape of dreams.

Maybe he's searching for someone he hasn't seen in a year.

• • •

Julia has a slice of time she doesn't think about. Probably everyone does, she tells herself. It's not as though the blacked-out squares in her mental calendar are weird or anything to worry about.

CHAPTER 6.

Every few weeks, little unexpected flashes of light from that era wake up Julia in the middle of the night. She gasps and sits up, sweat prickling the back of her neck, and remembers how her mother wore her hair, twisted up in a messy bun. Sometimes she tied a scarf backwards with the knot over one eyebrow so she looked like a woman from the 1940's.

She laughed a lot too, although her humor was subtle and dry. When she talked during dinner, the light from the overhead chandelier kissed the smooth brown skin of her brow marked only by a musical staff of wrinkles.

"Wrinkles!" Ghost huffs. "Don't even. You weren't supposed to see."

"Think I'm getting them?" Julia rubs her thumb over her forehead. She hears a light giggle before Ghost tells her to quit her nonsense and turn off the light.

"Sleep," Ghost adds. "You've got a big day tomorrow."

CHAPTER 7.

Bash is already at work inside the barn when Julia arrives, sanding the edges of a flat board. "Can you grab Harley?" he asks in place of a hello. "The sawdust isn't good for her."

The guinea pig is draped around his neck, tooting mournfully into Bash's collar. As soon as Julia reaches for the animal, Harley becomes a coiled spring of wound energy and he hunches his shoulders. "Ouch! Damn, she's got sharp claws. Time for a trim."

Julia carries Harley to the long, open cage. The guinea pig appears to decide Julia is trustworthy and relaxes against her chest. When she runs her fingertips over the soft, orange fur under the animal's neck, she's rewarded with a trembling purr. It's addictive to stand in the dusty streams of sunlight and stroke the little creature.

"Come help me sand these?" Bash calls out.

"Okay." Julia retrieves the limp parsley she brought from a baggie. She gives a piece to Harley, who begins to munch right away, eyeing Julia suspiciously around the green frills.

"I cut out most of the pieces last night," Bash announces when she joins him at the work table. "I think they'll fit together – hope so, anyway." He caresses one edge marked with angled scallops. "See? I snuck in a few dovetails to make it really secure. Five-year-old kids can be rough on wood projects. I was a tornado when I was a kid, so trust me on this."

Julia measures his calm demeanor, the way he sands the wood as though he has nothing more important to do. "I find that hard to believe," she says, accepting another piece of wood and a square of fine sandpaper.

"It's true. I was a brat. Just running around, getting into trouble all the time. Hey, want a pair of gloves to protect your nails or skin or whatever?"

With a short laugh, Julia shows him her hands, nails chopped as short as possible. She doesn't have time for manicures, and her job at Aggie's would make it a waste. Bash seems to approve, head ducking over the edge he works on. "Did you go out last night?" she asks.

His glance looks like Harley's suspicious glare. "I told you, I was on the jigsaw in my basement. It takes a while to get the measurements exact."

"I just don't want to take up all your social life." She accepts a piece of scratchy sandpaper and begins to move it against the wood.

Bash's long, warm fingers fold over hers. "Shorter strokes," he advises. "Work the sandpaper into the corners by folding it. If we can make it smooth now it'll be easier to put together and more waterproof." Julia copies his movements, and his eyebrows twitch together. "Besides, I'm not really into parties."

"No?"

"No," he answers in a grim tone. "I don't drink."

"Okay." She works on the slanted edge he's given her, the side of the tiny house. The wood is dry but yielding to the sandpaper. It's a repetitive task, but at least she can breathe in the barn without feeling as though she's drowning.

"Let's give it a try." Bash runs his thumb over the edge she's been sanding and hums in approval. He holds it up to his piece, and the two edges slot together perfectly. "Nice," he adds, a small sigh of satisfaction. "We'll put in glue joints and tarpaper the top before we paint the whole thing. You know, give it a few levels of protection so your books don't turn to mush in rain and snow and all that."

Julia takes another piece and starts to sand it. "Why'd you give Isaac a job?" Bash asks. She has the idea he keeps his gaze on the wood so he won't have to look at her.

"He begged and I caved."

"Isaac's an annoying asshat," Bash growls.

"But he's a good person underneath all that spiky hair," Julia protests. "Plus, it must be tough to be – to be what he is…"

He snorts. "Yeah, really tough. Two parents with good jobs, both giving him everything he wants, and he repays them by trashing their house once a week."

Julia thinks of her dad hiding inside since her mom passed away, growing paler and smaller each year. She gets the anger, but Isaac's life isn't perfect either. "Maybe he needs someone to talk to."

The square, brown hand holding the sandpaper moves faster, brushing the wood with quick swipes. "And you're it? You're his buddy now?"

Julia faces him, puts one fist on her hip. "Maybe I am." She turns away and clears her throat. "Hey, is parsley okay for guinea pigs? I brought some for Harley. Should have checked first."

"Yeah, she loves that stuff."

She snaps her fingers. "I need to check with the permit office, make sure the paperwork still is good with the new structure. Better write to Hillman Minx again, too. Guess I can't do any of that today, huh? I'll have to wait 'til Monday." It's all just noise. The question she really wants to ask seems to be stuck in her throat.

"Can you come back here tomorrow before all the admin stuff heats up?" He launches into professional mode and plans for the next stage of building the box: assembly, glue, and trim.

"It's Sunday, which means brunch at the diner…"

"Call Isaac and have him take your shift since you have back-up now." His matter-of-fact tone makes it seem so simple.

Julia does the usual mental arithmetic. Ride her mom's old bike instead of driving the truck, steal soup from the fridge to bring to school for lunch, skip a month of stashing away money for her dwindling dream of college…

She can make it happen. "Okay." It's a good idea, and it'll make everything go more smoothly. "I should update Hillman Minx."

"Hillman Minx," Bash scoffs. "I take it that's a pseudonym?"

"It's an early Isuzu car model," Julia explains. "I think he meant it to be ironic."

"Makes him sound like a douche."

She decides to change the subject. "What do you do on the weekends if you're not into parties?"

"I've got a lot going on." He didn't elaborate. "Got to keep the barn from falling down."

Julia fingers the sandpaper and remembers the box in the cupboard with diamond partitions. "Do you create stuff on your own? Make your own projects? You know, like the hinged box you showed me."

It earns her another secret smile. His teeth are sharp, angled slightly outwards as though he's wolf who's ready to bite. "Maybe. I can show you when you come here instead of working at Aggie's Diner tomorrow."

Julia grins into her sandpaper. "It's a big sacrifice," she sighs. "Brunch is a lot of fun at the diner – the spilled maple syrup, the mountain of coffee filters, and of course scrubbing out the toilets is always a joyful experience…"

He nudges her shoulder. "I can offer coffee and conversation with the hog."

"I'll bring more fresh veggies. Maybe Harley will start to trust me after a few more visits."

They lapse into easy silence, weightless as the streams of sunshine from the high barn windows.

• • •

"What are you doing tonight?" Bash asks as he walks her back to the truck.

"Chemistry," Julia groans. "I have to come up with something for Fry's essay." The assignment hangs over her, an impossible task. "I think I did okay on the test, thanks to you, and if I can turn in a good paper my grade might come up. And of course, I owe you that A."

She's used to his scowl by now. It doesn't always mean anger, just deep thought. As he opens her door and leans in over the window, he tells her she should have brought homework to do in the barn.

"I'll bring it tomorrow," Julia offers as she climbs into the cab.

"That works. I'll have that coffee I promised, maybe some donuts if the stars align. Tell you what, I'll set up some chairs and bring out a table so we can really get to work."

She can picture it, the two of them bent over essays in the abandoned stables, Harley wheeling for attention as she and Bash balance equations and write about modern advancements in chemistry. It's a peaceful image. Hanging out with Bash has been a new, quiet thread in her life, one she never could have imagined. In place of the loud partier she expected, he's a calm presence.

Solid.

Strong.

He leans in through the window, and for a moment Julia thinks he's going for a kiss. Her lashes flutter down, but instead he cups her neck in one broad, warm palm. "Your little house is going to be beautiful, Julia," he says. "We'll make it amazing."

His dark hair is long enough for one strand to frame the strong line of his jaw. On a whim Julia reaches out and tucks it back behind his ear. The skin of his neck is surprisingly soft, and he shivers slightly before slapping the side of her truck and stepping back.

The driveway is nothing more than a gravel track nearly lost among the tall grass. Wilderness is encroaching on the barn, with white butterflies hopping among the yarrow and asters. In the summer it's probably a great place to watch fireflies.

Julia reverses down the drive, twists to look out the tiny back window with one hand on the passenger seat. The drive is long, since the barn is set back from the road and she has to be careful to stay on the gravel.

As she pulls out onto the deserted avenue, she sees Bash's actual house. The deep porch is swept and empty of furniture. Thick curtains cover all the windows – no shafts of late sunshine in there.

He hasn't invited her inside yet.

She takes one last look in her rearview mirror, hoping to catch a final glimpse of Bash as he carries his tools back to the house. Instead Julia catches movement at one of the upstairs windows. The curtain is thrust back, and a face appears at the glass. A trick of the sun on the mirror makes it seem malevolent, almost alien, and Julia's breath catches in her throat.

The truck whines as she shifts gear. Already the face is gone, and the windows are shrouded once more behind the heavy drapes.

CHAPTER 8.

Isaac agrees to cover the brunch shift when Julia calls him. Of course, he gets all dramatic about it and insists she owes him her firstborn.

"No way. The experience and on-the-job training alone pay you back."

He's easy to talk to, and she finds herself smiling as she clicks off the phone and plucks the truck keys and phone from the little table beside her bed. "Lipstick? Mascara?" Ghost suggests.

"I'm going to a barn, not a club."

Her dad's slumped in front of the computer typing in a half-hearted manner when she emerges from her bedroom. Julia stops by his chair, and he swivels to squint up at her. "Going to work?"

"Heading over to a friend's house. We're rebuilding the Little Free Library."

He tips his head back. "Good for you. Mom's stubborn, just like you. I guess it's in the genes."

"Being stubborn isn't always good. Also, she's not here." His chair rocks as if she's hit him, and Julia decides she might as well keep going. "Want to come with me and see? Get out of the house."

"Oh. Out. No, I don't – no. No, you go and have fun. I mean, work. Work is what I meant. I mean, I have to work too, which is what I'm doing! Of course!"

Julia stoops and kisses him on one prickly cheek. "Don't just eat soup today," she says. "I brought home bread from the diner the other night – pie too."

"Pie, huh?" His voice fills with wonder. "It's a long time since I've had a slice of pie."

"I think it's cherry." Julia raises and lowers her eyebrows. "Okay if I clean up mom's old bike and use it? I have to save gas money."

Her dad jerks away from her touch and sits down to type. "Might be a pump by the bike stand," he tells the computer screen. Of course he has to spoil it by adding, "Better ask her first, though."

• • •

Julia coasts down the shallow dip leading to Bash's driveway and turns into the weed-clotted tracks before she dismounts. The ground is pitted and filled with rocks, making it impossible to navigate on a bike. Her backpack hangs heavily off her shoulders, and the baggie filled with vegetables for Harley nearly falls from her pocket.

As she wheels squeakily past the house it's completely silent. Nothing moves at any of the windows. There's an extra car in the driveway, so maybe Bash's parents are home. If so, there's no other sign of their existence.

By the time she reaches the barn she's sweating. The sun bakes her shoulders, although steelhead clouds clump along the tree line. Julia leans the bike against one of the barn timbers holding up the hayloft and walks into the cool, darkened interior.

Someone's talking in a low voice. Julia remembers the face she saw at the window upstairs. Probably it was one of Bash's parents or a sister, and now they're visiting him in the barn as he works on Julia's project. She swats at the hair on her face with one wrist and walks into the tiny space, ready to meet his family.

There's a moment when everything changes, when the day becomes something different from what you've planned or imagined. Julia sees Bash leaning over the pieces they sanded, intent on fitting them together. Beside him London props her elbows on the tool bench as she scrolls through something on her phone. She wears a short skirt, jeweled flip-flops, and a soft leather jacket hugs the curves of her chest.

Julia steps back, and her sneaker scuffs the wooden plank floor. Both London and Bash look up and see her in all her messy, sweaty glory.

"Sorry," Julia begins before she realizes she has nothing to apologize for. Bash was the one who invited her, after all.

Bash waves her over. "Come take a look. I think we can get the whole box together by this evening and actually reinforce the inside this week. If we can paint it by Friday, we're good to go for your opening day." One corner of his mouth quirks into its usual amused crescent.

"Oh." Julia has no idea what to do. London is standing in the spot where Julia usually hangs out, and she feels dumb standing in the doorway. "So. That's good."

"I actually have a surprise for you. Rigged it up last night." His dark eyes light up, and he puts down the corner he's holding. It's the floor and two walls of the box. "I left it in the basement, though."

"Okay." Julia takes a step to follow him, but London moves to wrap her hand around Julia's bicep.

"We'll wait here," she calls. His footsteps pad away, and London adds, "You don't want to go into his house. Trust me."

Julia pulls away from the girl, and her baggie filled with cucumbers, lettuce, and green peppers falls to the ground. London swoops in a graceful arc and picks it up. "For Harley? C'mon, let's feed her." Ignoring Julia's protest, she stalks to the guinea pig's cage.

Harley is already wheeking by the bars. "Here you go, piggy," London says. She kneels and offers a wilted leaf of romaine to Harley. The guinea pig munches the lettuce, looking like a dancer in a musical who's decided to eat her frilly fan.

After the conversation with her dad, a confrontation with London makes Julia feel like an unwanted accessory. Anger boils up when she thinks she could be at Aggie's Diner making gas money, surrounded by cheerful noise and the clatter of dishes. Anywhere would be better than squatting next to London feeding Harley with Julia's vegetables.

"I'm sorry about your mom."

"What?" Julia jerks her head, startled.

"She's dead, right?" London plucks out a carrot and tosses it into Harley's hay.

Cautiously Julia crouches by the cage. Harley snuffles, intent on the carrot. "Guess no one ever accused you of not getting right to the point."

London dusts off her hands and looks directly at Julia. In the sliced sunlight her eyes are pale green, striking against her tanned skin. "My dad's ex-military and insisted on raising me to be hard, so I'm not exactly PC. You can tell me to fuck off, though."

Julia tips her head to one side. "She was killed by a drink driver."

"Oh, well that sucks." London twists the bag, now empty.

"She bled out in the ambulance. Never made it to the hospital. So that Little Free Library I've been working on for months would be a memorial. You know?" Julia has no idea why she's saying this to London, of all people.

"I get it." London turns away from the cage. "Oh hey, sounds like Bash is back. Come on." She stands and, surprisingly, holds out a hand to help Julia to her feet.

"Check it out," Bash says without preamble as he enters. He's holding up a flat piece of metal trailing wires. "I found this old solar panel among my grandfather's stuff, and it still works. I'm going to wire it to the roof of the box and attach an LED light."

"What's to stop someone from just ripping off the light? And the books? And the box itself?" London demands.

Julia catches Bash's eye, one brow raised. "It could happen," she confesses. "Like the jackass who crashed into my first box the moment I got it up. But once the library's installed and people use it, maybe they'll see it belongs to them too. I mean, the concept is to take a book and leave a book. If it's their stuff inside, it belongs to everyone, really."

"Julia, hold this while I measure the roof," Bash says.

London pulls out her phone and instantly returns to the persona Julia knows from school and Isaac's party – prickly, unfriendly. "Sounds like pass the Kool-Aid if you ask me."

"I didn't ask you," Julia argues as she takes the metal piece. "And it's already working, right now, in thousands of locations worldwide. There are places where kids can't find books at all – the LFL group calls them 'book deserts.' Sometimes these boxes are all they have."

"Huh," Bash murmurs. He aligns the solar panel with the piece in Julia's hands and nods. "Yup, this is going to work." The two components slot together perfectly.

"I have to go," London declares. Stashing her phone in her back pocket, she leans over and gives Bash a kiss on his cheek.

"Wait. I'll walk you out." Julia follows London, ignoring Bash's curious frown. When they reach the timbers, she blows the curls out of her face. "Hey, thanks for listening. About my mom."

London shrugs, and her pale eyes assess Julia face as though they're back in Mr. Fry's class waiting for the lesson to begin. "You can talk to other people, you know."

"I know. It's just my dad has a hard time with it. In fact, he won't admit to himself that she's gone."

"Why did you tell me?"

"You asked."

"Huh. Okay. Well, I'm out." London's boot heels crunch over the graveled driveway before she climbs into her car and fusses with her bangs in the rearview mirror. Julia watches for a minute before turning away.

When she reenters the barn, Bash is still working on the solar panel. He looks up and puts his soldering iron on the tool bench, rubs the back of his neck, and screws his mouth into an embarrassed shape. "I didn't know she was coming over," he says. "Also, I didn't have time to get coffee and donuts for us."

Julia runs her finger over the surface of the solar panel. "It's fine," she says. "I'm not going to freak out over another girl being here while we work on a miniature house. Nice job with the solar panel, by the way. Where did you get it? How much did it cost? Oh! I nearly forgot. We still need to talk about what I owe you for your time."

"How about we both shut up for a second?" His warm, wide palm is gentle against her cheek.

Outside London's car starts up. Bash waits, not moving, until the sounds of her engine dies away. The tiny room is dark and warm as the chamber of a heart.

Julia hears her own heart beating, a hammer against a brass hinge.

His eyes never leaving hers, Bash leans forward. His mouth slants over hers, a brief and delicious kiss. His breath is warm, tongue soft against her lower lip.

When he straightens, Julia realizes he's trembling.

It's as though Bash is forcing himself to be quiet. As though he holds himself back from the brink of a cliff where he and Julia are about to take flight in a soaring dive to blue sea and razor rocks below the surface of the waves.

CHAPTER 9.

Julia has no idea how everything will go after the kiss in the barn. But still. It's a glowing memory, and her blood races when she thinks of it as she bikes to school, as she eats her lunch, while she works on math problems.

However, Bash's chair is empty when she gets to chemistry class. "He stayed home," London announces as soon as Julia sits at their table. "Damn, 14 percent power. Are you kidding me?" She scowls at the screen of her phone.

"Is he sick?" Julia asks.

"You could say that." London's tone is distracted as she settles back in her seat. "Finish your little project?"

"No." After the kiss in the barn, Bash returned to the pieces of wood as though nothing had changed. The rest of the day passed as though he and Julia were in a synchronized swim routine. They swam around each other perfectly, the sounds of the tools and faraway traffic muted, before she reluctantly left him and biked home. "I wanted to try and put it up this week. But it looks like it won't happen."

Julia's about to say more, but Mr. Fry calls for their homework. Hers is miraculously complete, written at the table Bash brought into the barn for their homework session. His paper is probably still in his pocket, folded into a careful square.

Class progresses with a group project. Julia's about to move to her customary place with two bored goths, when London calls out to Fry. "Can Julia work with my group today?"

The teacher opens his mouth to argue, but London beckons him with a slow roll of her fingers and says something into his ear Julia can't understand. Mr. Fry's lips harden, but he waves Julia over.

London's group is lively. One of the guys immediately starts teasing London as soon as the girls sit down. "Here's my future wife," he starts.

"In your dreams. Say hi to Julia," London orders, and they chorus

Hello, Julia.

It's like being in a playroom. The guys knock each other's elbows as they write, although they concentrate on the questions Mr. Fry has handed out. Their conversation winds in and out of the past weekend, the upcoming football draft, and the best way to figure out chemical equations. They're the athletic type of kids Julia never hangs out with, simply because she's never considered it as a possibility.

Their sports jackets flap over broad chests. When one of the guys twists to get a pen out of his backpack, Julia can read the machine embroidery on the back: *Varsity Lacrosse.*

To her surprise, Julia finds herself relaxing. She's able to sit back and watch London flirt with the Lacrosse Twins, which is almost better than a movie. At the end of the class, their group hands in a completed set of papers with responses that aren't totally horrible.

Throughout the entire class Bash's chair remains empty.

• • •

Julia bikes home through a sudden spring downpour. By the time she reaches the garage, water covers the pedals of the bike. Julia pushes up the screeching door, wheels her mom's bike in beside the truck, and shoves down the kickstand.

Julia finds an old towel and dries off the bike before she remembers her books and papers in the sopping backpack. The zipper sticks, and she wrestles it open to find pages warped with rain.

Arms filled with disorganized schoolwork and the Little Free Library plans, Julia brings them into the tiny mudroom and spreads the stuff across the floor to dry out. Her soaked sneakers go into the sink, and her sweatshirt on a hook in the garage.

Thinking of showers and maybe her dad's soup, Julia walks into the living room and stops. Her father stands there, surrounded by a starburst of litter and dust. "Sorry," he says helplessly. "Thought I'd clean up, and the vacuum cleaner exploded." Although his hairline has receded, his pale skin looks soft, unlined. Probably all the time inside is keeping him young.

Julia sucks in a breath. As she eyes the disaster, there's a blue rifting crash in the sky. The lightning is jagged as the edge of a key.

All the lights in the house instantly blink out.

"Julia," her father says plaintively. "Julia, can you help me find the broom?"

She feels it's all too much. The lightning, vacuum cleaner, and her useless father are like blows of a hammer driving a nail into red cedar.

"Check the hall closet." Julia goes to her room, strips out of her soaked clothes, and slumps on the bed. Her wet skin is cold, then hot. Breath catches in her throat, and she feels a familiar fight for breath.

Panic attack. Julia hasn't had one since… She shakes her head, willing away the memory of that tragic night, and picks up her phone. For a moment her finger hovers over Bash's contact, but she doesn't want to be that needy girl who latches on.

Julia wills her heart to slow in her chest until the black spots clear from her vision. When she can breathe again, she powers down her phone.

"You still have me," Ghost reminds her.

Yeah, Julia thinks. *I still have you.*

If she doesn't do something, Julia feels she'll stay inside the house forever. Of course, there's always one person who wants to see her, and after wrestling with her conscience, she gives Isaac a call.

"Want to go and check out the park like we talked about?" Julia says as soon as he picks up.

"Really?" His voice slides up an octave. "You really mean it?"

• • •

"That was the slowest Lyft driver ever," Isaac declares when she backs the truck out of the garage and he climbs into the passenger seat. "Give me a ride home after?"

"Sure." Julia eyes him, all sparkly in the arrows of sun through wet leaves. "But you owe me for gas then."

"I wouldn't have it any other way." His grin is filled with mischief. "You won't believe this, but I used to come to this park all the time for soccer practice. First town leagues when I was just a sprout, then school, then travel. Every day before dinner, sometimes after as well."

Julia's truck sluices into the capillary roads of Blue Anchor Park. *Just a few days ago,* she thinks, *I was installing the library book shelf in this park. If I had waited, I wouldn't be here now. I probably wouldn't be hanging with Isaac. I'd be home with Dad and... and the empty bedroom.*

"So how about that?" Ghost murmurs. "Would that have been better or worse?"

Probably there's no good answer to that question. "I don't know." Julia darts a look at Isaac to see if he's heard her, but he's still talking about soccer.

"I scored two goals in the final game I played," he finishes. "Gave it up after that, no idea why. Tiffany rags me about it all the time."

Julia breaks and opens the door. "The crash happened here."

Isaac forgets about soccer and tumbles out after her. "We should have brought flashlights and stuff."

"And a magnifying glass? And deerstalker hats?" The night air is cool and feels good on Julia's skin as she kneels next to the pavement. "Here's the exact spot where the car hit my project."

"What kind of car?"

She shakes her head. "It happened so fast that I couldn't even get a look, let alone grab the license plate number."

The tiny patch of ground is deserted, feeling breathless in the quiet afternoon. Julia stands up and runs both hands through her curls. "This is useless. We're wasting our time."

"Wait." Isaac squats next to her and feels the pavement. "Can you turn on your headlights? There's something here."

Julia reaches over Ghost, who's slumped over the wheel to watch, and switches on the lights. In their gleam, Isaac looks like an anime figure coiled into a C beside the road, feeling the pavement with one thumb.

"Yeah." He beckons her over and points to the cement. "See right here? Someone's been messing with this. It's all chipped, except for this section."

Isaac is right. When Julia feels the sidewalk, there's a small portion that's smooth. It feels as if someone has sanded it carefully – a strange thing to do, probably an act done in secret.

The blood rushes away from her head when she stands in a dizzy rush. Julia waits for the sky to stop swinging around her.

She feels dirty all of a sudden, as though she'd been caught with both hands inside a medicine chest or a private jewelry box.

CHAPTER 10.

Dear Ms. Craniver, Julia writes. She considers the phrase floating on the word doc and erases the first word. *Ms. Craniver, I wanted to update you and Mr. Minx on the status of the Little Free Library opening you agreed to attend. Despite some setbacks, we are on schedule to open the first library box in New Jersey on the agreed date, the first Saturday in May at 11 am. Please let me know if you need anything else for the opening ceremony.*

She adds her name and rereads the email. After chewing her nail, she changes 'setbacks' to 'challenges.' It sounds official enough to get through D. Craniver's vigorous demands.

Before hitting Send, she calls for her dad. His voice is rumpled with sleep, and when he walks into her room he's tying his old, brown robe with one hand as he scratches his cheek with the other. "Read this and let me know what you think," Julia asks. "I have to send it off today."

The stubble catches her ear as he leans over her shoulder to look at the email. "Looks good," he says, and his chapped lips curve slightly downwards in his version of a smile. "How did you get all grown up so suddenly?"

The chair squeaks as she swivels to face him. "Grown up? You really think so?"

"Yeah. I really do." He stands up and shoves both hands in the pockets of the old robe. "You know, Julia…"

The morning air is charged with the things they never say to each other. "If you can make it to the Library opening, great," she says. "If you don't, well – not gonna lie. I'll be disappointed."

"That'll make two of us." His voice is so quiet she can barely hear him, and she has the sudden terrifying thought he's slowly unraveling like a sweater. Pull on a loose thread and he'll end up as a pile of crinkly yarn.

Who will save him, she wonders, *when I finally move out?*

• • •

Julia locks up her mom's bike at the school's stand, empty except for a few Schwinn models. She smells timothy hay and, when she turns, Bash is close enough to feel the electrons of heat spiraling out of his skin. His hands are warm on her waist, and she slides one arm around his neck. "Where were you yesterday? During school, I mean."

Bash is as solid as ever. She feels his strength, the way his muscles slide under smooth, brown skin as he deliberately folds his palm against the small of her back. "Had to do something," he says. "Couldn't get out of it. I was able to put your house together, though."

She likes the way he says 'your house.' The words make her project seems like more than a glorified box for other people's books. "You missed some fascinating group projects."

"Oh damn."

Julia knows he's glad to see her. They've been friends for such a short time, and already she understands him inside and out.

"You still have to work on Fry's essay to pay off your huge debt to me." Bash's words are muffled in her shoulder, but she can tell he's smiling.

They walk into the school building together, Julia's hip bumping against his muscled thigh. She juggles her bike-lock keys, and Bash pulls out one of the paper squares from his right pocket.

Julia listens as he describes the house, details the next steps of starting in on tarpaper and paint as early as the evening. "Can you come to my barn this afternoon?" Bash adds.

"I have to work." Julia looks into his eyes, dark and damaged as if he's constantly expecting disappointment. "My shift ends at 7, though. I can probably bike over before it gets too dark." She has to earn enough money to pay back Isaac for the gas. It's what her life has become, a constant scramble to stay ahead of her debts.

"Okay. I'll save the most boring tasks for you." One blunt fingertip along her jaw, and he's gone.

That contact warms her through several classes until lunch. She's hidden in one corner so she can finish an assignment on the subjunctive mood for Spanish, when her phone yelps with the sound of an incoming email. Idly she glances at her phone and sees the message is from D. Craniver, a response to Julia's request for more time.

The disorganization surrounding this event is completely unacceptable.

You understand we work with a very tight schedule. Already Mr. Minx has several engagements lined up for that date. I regret to inform you he is therefore unable to attend the opening of your Little Free Library in Blue Anchor.

If you had written earlier we could have made room for you, but at this late date we must decline your invitation. In the future, please organize your communication further in advance.

Julia reads the email several times. The words hover in virtual space, a cold assessment of time and responsibility: proof she's failed once again.

The granola bar she shoved in her backpack last minute is cold and unappetizing. After a few bites Julia gets up and throws it away.

No one else realizes what a screw-up she is. Spanish is a blur, and American History is the same. They're assigned a presentation and given a quiz on the Vietnam War. For a wonder she actually knows the material, thanks to her study sessions in the barn with Bash and Harley. Her stomach flops with nerves and anger but she makes it through the long afternoon.

We must decline.

Further in advance.

Completely unacceptable.

A white rectangle lies on her desk when she enters Chemistry, the test from the week before. "Not bad," Fry says when she sits in her desk. "Not bad at all."

Julia lifts the corner of her test to peek at the grade as Bash slides into his seat, raises his chin inquiringly. "Well?"

An A is written in red on the top left corner, and mutely she holds it out so he can see it. "Nice," Bash says. Julia nods, and he leans closer just as London comes in. "What's wrong?" he whispers.

"Can you at least save the make-out session for later?" London snaps. She tosses a lemon curl over one shoulder.

Bash ignores her. "What?"

Julia digs out her phone and shows him the email from D. Craniver. She can't keep her hands from shaking as she holds up the screen. "Maybe I wrote too late. I just wanted to make sure the Little Free Library would be ready, you know? It would be totally embarrassing if a famous poet came to open something and it wasn't ready. Right? But she says..."

"What? No way. Not happening. Just give me one second with this Craniver bitch." Julia watches as Bash takes her phone and types something onto the screen. A moment later Julia hears a tinny hunting horn, the mail-sent alert she's set on the phone.

"What did you do?" she protests. Bash just hands back her phone and gives Julia one of his secret smiles.

"Hanging out tonight?" London interrupts, leaning towards him. "I'll come over later."

"Can't, sorry. I need to work on Julia's Library project."

The girl doesn't know how to speak his language, Julia realizes, that special Bash-speak rich with hidden clues and mystery. Although they're obviously old friends, London doesn't understand the intricate dovetails of Bash's personality.

Her eyes dart between Bash and Julia and, when Fry calls for the groups to get together, London gets up and goes to plunk down next to the Lacrosse Twins. "Are you with them?" Mr. Fry asks Julia.

"It was just for one day," London says.

"Yes." As she gets up, Bash puts his palm on Julia's lower back and guides her to the group. "She's with us."

"Yeah," one of the Lacrosse Twins echoes. "Julia's our lucky charm now."

• • •

Between the history presentation, Chem essay, and upcoming exams, Julia feels she's barely started her homework before it's time to head to Aggie's diner. She plops her backpack in the break room in case she has a few moments to work on valance formulas and write up ideas for her essay.

Ben and Aggie are already arguing when she enters the kitchen. "I said take it for a walk around the yard, not cover it in five pounds of onions." Aggie scribbles something on her pad and rips the paper off with a determined whoosh. She and Bash would probably get along.

Ben grunts. "Don't see why you can't just talk like a normal person. It's the new millennium, not World War 2." Aggie flounces out of the kitchen, unsuccessfully trying to slam the swing door, and Ben frowns at her departing butt before wheeling to face Julia. "What are you scowling about?"

"That was really mean," Julia says. "And you know it."

He scrapes off the grease from his grill with unnecessary vigor. Julia ties her apron and picks up a tray of ketchup bottles. Just as she shoulders open the door, she hears his answer: "Yeah. Maybe you're right."

• • •

Julia's phone blats out its hunting horn alert for a new email. She swipes the screen sees it's an extremely brief message from D. Craniver. *We will find room in our schedule for Mr. Minx to visit Blue Anchor on the previously agreed time and date.*

She doesn't move for a few minutes. In the diner, there's the usual midweek lull. Several people order the early special. Two women talk earnestly over coffee and pie, and a lone trucker in flattened cap and loose jeans wolfs down a burger.

Among the nighthawks, Julia feels a rare throb of happiness. Somehow, in that moment when he took her phone and inserted himself into the Hillman Minx conversation, Bash has tamed D. Craniver.

But it's dinner hour, and she has no time to celebrate. Unable to hide her grin, Julia picks up her busser's tray and sails into the dining room, feeling like a victorious warship. At the end of her shift, things kick into high gear. A table of priests order huge meals with extra desserts and leave a large tip. Several families come in and sit at the bar, and a rowdy group of athletes arrive, all thirsty and starving after a game.

When it's busy like this, Julia rushes each table. The quicker turnaround means higher tips for everyone, which is good, but also a lot more work across the board. Aggie delivers oval plates to a couple sitting on top of each other while Julia cleans the corner table. As she picks up shredded food and dropped fries after a family with two kids and a baby, someone behind the padded seat says her name.

Bash is in the booth, facing a milkshake and a half-eaten patty melt. "The food's good," he says.

"Best burgers in five states, honey." Aggie writes rapidly on her pad and hands him his check before heading back to the kitchen. Maybe she's going to yell at Ben again.

Julia plops her wet rag into the basin filled with coffee saucers and oval plates before balancing it on one hip. "Don't tell me you're here for the patty melt."

"Nope. Want a ride? Figured we could save time that way and get some studying done."

"I still have to Bissell and finish the sugar shakers, not to mention the ketchup…"

"You go along." Aggie reappears and undoes the bow of Julia's apron with one quick tug. "Here, don't forget your tips."

Julia protests she has to get her backpack, and Aggie follows her into the kitchen where Ben gives them a wary look but says nothing. "Your fella out there…" Aggie starts.

"He's not my fella."

"Not sure he got that memo." Aggie digs in her pocket and hands over a wad of carefully folded bills. "Here you go. Nice hustle tonight. And while you're having your little chat, ask him what he's thinking." And when Julia frowns, confused, Aggie jerks her head in the direction of the dining room. "People like him are dark horses."

She swats Ben on his papery, tented hat as he hoots at Aggie's choice of words. "What I'm saying is this – shadowy guys like him have secrets, honey."

• • •

"I thought we could take Harley outside for a snack," Bash suggests when they park in his gravelly driveway. Julia nods and follows him into the barn, where they flounder back through the empty stalls to Harley's cage. He scoops up the guinea pig and settles her over his collarbone.

Taking a long breath, Julia makes the final decision to ask the question that's been bugging her for hours. "What exactly did you say in the email you sent?" Bash is walking in front of her, heading out the back of the barn to a small field filled with yellow and blue flowers.

"What email? Look, Harley loves the dandelions here." Bash sits and spreads his legs, indicates to Julia she should do the same thing. They form a human diamond to contain the snuffly guinea pig. Harley hops with excitement before she reels a dandelion stalk like stiff spaghetti into her mouth with rapid chews. "Hog," he adds with grumpy affection. "Just have to make sure a hawk doesn't fly off with her, although they usually are gone after sundown. Still, we need to be careful."

"Oh, wow. Okay." Julia leans forward as if she could protect the animal with her body. "And you already know what I mean. The email you sent today on my phone to the D. Craniver lady. It worked, by the way."

"It did?" Bash looks up, a bright smile carving his face. She's never seen him so relaxed.

"It did." Julia holds out her fingers, and Harley runs over to sniff her thumb and swipes the end with a rough tongue. "Bash, look! I'm getting piggy kisses."

"Let's just say I can be pretty convincing when the need arises." He leans back on his wrists and displays the line of his throat in a challenge.

Julia eyes him for a moment before taking out her phone and swiping to the email app, but he must have already deleted his original message

THE EXQUISITE CHEMISTRY OF BLOOD

from the Sent folder. "Damn it!"

The only hint he's laughing is his eyes, changing shape from suspicious almonds to glittery crescents. Julia can feel the seat of her jeans getting damp from the afternoon's rain, but she doesn't care – it's nice to sit in the dark field as Harley eats her snack. "We should check out the project," she says, itching her cheek. "Probably do some homework too. It's nearly ten o'clock."

"We will. Just a few more minutes." His boot presses against the sole of her sneaker, a thread of connection. They reach out for the guinea pig at the same time, stroke the small, furry jellybean. Around them the field is alive with moths and outraged tree frogs.

His fingers lap hers and slot them together. Under their touch Harley quivers in a violent purr. "She likes you too," Bash says.

A cry splits the air, and the guinea pig popcorns with fright. The shout sounds like a prisoner about to walk into Death Row.

Bash spits out a thread of curses and jumps up. "I have to go. Keep an eye on Harley." Without another word he strides towards the barn.

"What the hell?" Ghost whispers. "That was weird, right? It's not just me?"

Julia gathers Harley into her arms, and the tiny animal trembles against her neck. Harley sniffs the air in his direction, probably wondering where her human went. Together, the girl and the guinea pig watch Bash as he strides into the great block of gray barn.

Wilma Rudolph might have walked with such decision as she entered the arena in the Roman heat of the 1960 Olympics. She must have looked down and gathered her thoughts before fitting her spikes against the starting blocks and prepared to sprint into the history books forever.

Shadowy. A guy with a secret, Julia thinks.

PART II
HURDLES

CHAPTER 11.

Bash knows exactly what has happened when he hears the scream. He trudges towards Nehi's house, the last place he wants to be. He'd give anything to be able to sit in the damp grass next to Julia and Harley all night.

Too bad. Suck it up, he tells himself.

The porch door is closed, but the well-oiled handle turns easily in his palm and the old hinges no longer squeak. Bash enters the kitchen and heads to the repurposed pantry so he can pick up his usual supplies.

The wooden floor shines in soft lamplight. Counters are bare of dishes and food. Everything is in its place, tidied away from the quick meal he ate earlier. The sink is empty. The faucet no longer drips after he replaced the washers a month ago.

All the usual supplies wait in the floor of the pantry: bucket, mop, and a bottle of spray cleanser he's mixed himself from a recipe he found online. Beside it there's a bag of clean rags cut from his old t-shirts and folded into neat squares.

Bash picks up the receiver of the old wall phone to make a quick call, but a thump from overhead makes him throw it down, dial tone buzzing like a wasps' nest. He doesn't bother to hang up.

The bucket bangs into his knee as he runs up the steps, hitting the bruise from last week when he went through the same process. Bash barely registers the pain. There's a series of mental steps he goes through each time along with getting supplies and bruises.

I can deal.

I've done this before.

I'm ready.

Maybe this time it won't be so bad.

And, new on the list: *Let me just finish and get back to the barn.*

The smell in the short, spare hallway tells him it's even worse than he expected. When he goes into Nehi's room, his mother lies in two puddles of lumpy fluids emerging from each end of her body.

Mop and bucket slap onto the floor. Working quickly, Bash removes his rags and cleanser. There's a thin blanket in the clothes bag, and he uses it to roll around Nehi so he can lift her.

Where'd you put it? he wants to scream. *Where'd you hide the liquor this time? Tell me so I can go and dump it out in the damn park again.*

There's no time. He has to get her cleaned up before he gets sick from Nehi's stink. Bash concentrates on getting her slumped, motionless weight into his arms and through the door into the bathtub.

He has retrofitted the tub to deal with her mess. Another bucket is ready to go under her chin, ready for a second deluge of vomit. The bathwater runs hot in seconds, thanks to the larger water-heater Bash installed last winter. Under its silver splash he's able to undress Nehi and throw her soiled pile of clothes into the bin he placed in the cabinet.

By this point he's working on autopilot. It's easier when he doesn't allow himself to feel pity, anger, or any emotion.

With quick, compact motions he hoses off Nehi's body and washes her sludge into a waste channel he developed. It leads out of the bathroom to a compost bin he built the summer of seventh grade after their toilet backed up for the fifth time.

The channel is a wide hose running off the tub through the walls of the house. It gurgles as the stuff sluices away, and Nehi's eyelids flutter. Maybe the noise, reminiscent of a giant dentist's suction tube, has roused her. Bash shoves the bucket closer to her chest as she heaves twice, three times, before voiding again.

More gurgles, more soap, more water. At this point he's dealt with the worst of it.

There's a handheld shower unit off the side of the tub. Bash rinses her again and gets her hair clean. It's thick and slick as wet tar on his wrist, shining black-silver from the cold light in the bathroom ceiling.

Nehi lies back against the porcelain, and Bash pulls down a folding support unit he designed to keep her upright so she won't drown in bath water or her own sputum. Once his mother's tiny body is secured, he's able to clean up the stinking brown oatmeal from the bedroom using first a shovel and then a mop.

At least the evening is warm enough to keep the windows open. Bash turns on the fan and scrubs the floor with his homemade cleanser, the only thing strong enough to deal with Nehi's shit and puke. It's easier to do now he's covered the upstairs wooden floorboards with linoleum.

As he swipes his mop under the bed, a glass vodka bottle rolls out and clinks at his knees like a grenade that has lost its pin.

The soiled rags and mop go back in the bucket. Bash returns to the tub, lets out the water, and rinses Nehi off one last time. She sags as he wraps towels around her and carries her back to the mattress lined with plastic sheets. There are bottles of water lined up neatly in the dresser, and he leaves a couple for her beside the bed.

The aspirin is in the locked medicine cabinet. Bash keeps the only key on his ring, but Nehi has tried to break it open before with a stolen hammer and, once, using her teeth.

Bash sprays more of his cleanser into the tub before striding to his room. His own soiled clothes go into the hamper. With quick motions he pulls on a new shirt and a clean pair of jeans.

The final step is to move his notes and papers from one set of pockets to another.

Bash returns to Nehi's room and looks around at gleaming linoleum and water bottles lined up in a neat row by her bed. The woman slumps on her side, another bucket ready in case sickness hits her again. She's as still as a corpse.

There's nothing else he can do.

• • •

Outside, Bash draws in great gulps of fresh air. The spring nights are still chilly, and he likes how the dark smells like hay and pine.

The hill is deserted, and a jittery thread of panic runs under his skin. For a moment he wonders if Julia grew tired of waiting. Maybe she finally got sick of him and called Uber. She could be heading to Isaac's house right now.

Just as he's about to shout, a soft sound filters from the barn. Limp with relief, he walks down the earthen horse ramp into the stall.

Julia sits beside Harley's cage, holding out a frond of hay. She looks up and smiles as he enters, and Bash feels his stomach flip at the sight of her bright grin and careless curls. "I thought I should bring Harley inside," she says. "We'd never find her if she got away in the dark."

Sit next to her, lean your head on her lap, put one arm around her waist. If he lets go of himself, Bash knows he'll lose the tight grip he keeps on his desire. Yet he can imagine how soft her thigh would feel under his neck, the way her fingers would twist in his hair. She would smell like smoke and salt.

To distract himself, Bash jerks his head in the direction of the tool-room. "Want to see our project?"

"Yeah." Julia gets up, stretches her back, and laughs. "I'm still stiff from work."

He holds out one hand. "C'mon, princess."

"Okay." Julia takes it and stops at the door of the tool-room. "Oh," she says so softly he can barely hear it. "Oh, Bash."

He lets go and, embarrassed, rubs his chest with one palm. "Turned out bigger than I thought with the solar panel and wiring."

Her lips form a soft O, and Bash can't help remembering how Julia's mouth tastes. "I wish…" She reaches out to touch the roofline.

Bash has built the bookshelf to resemble a double-story house complete with windows, rooms, and an upstairs balcony. There isn't much detail since the turnaround time has been so short, but maybe later he'll be able to add a tiny set of steps or a fancy frame around the door.

Inside there are two shelves, both reinforced to bear the weight of donated books.

"There's space for the license and Free Library tag above the door, here. I've weather-stripped the inside, plus it's magnetized so some doofus won't leave the thing hanging open and ruin all the books, like we talked about before, right? Here's the light, attached to this solar panel." He points to an LED bulb, which he's wired to look like a lantern protected behind a grille so no one can walk off with it. "And I thought maybe…" Her nose wrinkles. Has Nehi's stink rubbed off on him? No, Julia seems more amused than disgusted. "The wood turned out okay. Here? And here? In fact, I thought we could varnish it instead of painting – leave it natural."

"It's a great idea. Besides, we have to show off that white birch." Julia goes on tiptoe to admire the joints.

"I have another surprise for you, but I'm not going to tell you yet."

This wins him her intent, blue gaze. "What is it? You can't just talk about surprises and not give me a hint."

He's got it all ready in the locked box inside the tool-room closet. She steps closer and tries to tickle his sides. "One hint. One."

"I'm not telling you!" he gasps.

"But you have to. I'm invested now."

He captures her hands, holds her fists between their chests. Around them the barn is warm and clean as outside the tree frogs start up a nighttime flirtation. "One hint," he says. "Just one, but you don't get to see it yet. Ready?"

"Yeah," she grins.

"Okay. Really ready?"

"Yes!" Laughter through her impatience.

"Julia, I'm going to make your house come alive."

• • •

They end up sitting on folding chairs in the barn, testing each other for various quizzes and working out what Julia will do for her presentation. After they finish studying, Bash grinds his way through a page of math. There's one answer to each problem, and it's relaxing to know he can solve something so definitively.

Almost by themselves, the chairs move closer together until he can feel the seam of Julia's jeans rub against the bruise where the bucket banged his leg on his way up the stairs. Each time she leans over to ask his advice or borrow an eraser, the slight twinge reminds him that she's actually here.

Bash draws out the work as long as possible, but at last the papers are all folded back into his pockets and her books are packed away. He helps her up and holds her hand on the way through the darkness to his Dart. In the front seat beside him the overhead light paints a stripe on her cheekbones and glances off her lovely curls.

He wants to navigate one-handed, his palm resting lightly on her knuckles, feeling the scars and calluses from too many shifts at the diner. However, maybe touch isn't necessary.

Julia talks as he drives the old car, commenting on stores they pass. *That gas station's been closed forever. Think someone's living inside? Maybe a family of possums? Hey, the ice cream shop's hiring. Maybe I can pick up a few extra hours.* Each word is another nail plastering her to his side, a stronger braid of the slender threads between them.

"What happens to us after your Little Free Library is finished?" The thought erupts from his chest, interrupting her idea to organize books over the weekend.

"Huh." Julia slumps against the seat. "Gotta admit I haven't thought about it. The whole thing's been so intense, you know? But we have the ceremony to get through first, as well as meeting Minx."

"The asshat," Bash growls.

"Yeah," she laughs. "But I guess you're talking about after it's all over, right?"

"Right."

Her backpack is at her feet, and Julia bounces one knee against it as she thinks. "Guess we'll just have to find another project."

She couldn't have possibly some up with a better answer.

Bash pulls up to her house, brakes, and shifts into Park. There's no awkward pause. Julia shifts right into his arms, brushes her lips over his, moves away. It's as though she knows exactly what he wants before he does.

"Pick you up before school tomorrow?" he asks. Julia blinks before saying that sounds good and she'll see him then.

He watches her climb out, heave her backpack over one shoulder, and walk up to her house. The lawn in front is pitted with neglect, and he imagines raking weeds, replanting the grass, adding a shade tree in a corner. The front door needs a new screen as well, and the steps lean drunkenly to one side. There are plenty of tasks to bind him and Julia together for weeks, months, years.

Bash relaxes against the faux leather of his seat and shifts into Drive.

• • •

The light puddles the second floor like a smashed birthday cake. It tells the story of what lies within even before Bash opens the car door and hears the cries, hoarse crows fleeing the neck of a broken bottle.

The Panic Kit is in the garage, hidden behind a string-bound pile of newspapers from 1993. Bash pulls out the box and opens it while he runs upstairs, his boots thudding on the treads.

Nehi stands in the middle of his bedroom. She's surrounded by Bash's socks and underwear strewn over the floor. "Where?" she demands. "Where'd you put it?"

To distract her, he points to the top shelf of his closet where t-shirts and sweats are stacked in neat piles. Nehi runs over and pulls a stack off so the clothes cascade around her. She manages to ruin most of Bash's organization before he can pull her arms together and click the handcuffs from his emergency stash around her wrists. The act is hateful and violent, a horrific violation of his nature.

Bash has no other choice. They've gone through this too many times. After each rampage, he's repaired the house. When Nehi found gasoline and threatened to torch the place if he didn't return her whiskey, Bash created his Panic Kit complete with handcuffs and a taser.

Getting her back to bed is like wrestling an alligator. The moment he snaps the second set of cuffs in place to anchor her to the metal post, Nehi freezes. "I gotta pee." Her crafty eyes follow him as he picks up her spilled water bottles.

"Do it in the bed. I already cleaned up your mess, one more won't make a difference."

Bash knows if he lets her go now she'll find a way to get outside, maybe pick the lock to his grandfather's closet and drink paint stripper or something worse. It's going to be well after midnight before he'll sleep.

He collapses against the wall in their hallway, pulls out his phone and punches the top contact. It rings a few times before a sleepy voice answers. "Bash?" A tiny rustle, a smothered cough. "Again? She did it again?"

"Can you come over?" He hates every part of this process.

There's a long intake of breath, and he forces himself not to beg. A mumbled Okay floats over the line, and he goes downstairs to wait.

• • •

London enters the house, marches through the kitchen, and flings her bag onto the entertainment center Bash made two years ago. "Jake's not around. He told me he'd come over ay ess ay pee." She frames his face with long fingers and looks into his eyes. "Bad one, huh? You look like hell."

If he talks about it, his careful exterior might crack. Instead, Bash just shrugs and steps back. "Is there any chance you can talk to her?"

"That's why I'm here. Right?" London walks up the stairs. He watches her go, his hands hanging uselessly by his side. After a moment he hears the door open, followed by hushed voices and the squeak of the bed as London sits next to Nehi.

Bash picks up a photo from the entertainment center. Its frame was one of the first wood projects he made with his grandfather's barn tools – Nehi's gift for a vanished Mother's Day. He was six when he nailed it together.

The knotty pine showcases a picture of two figures in chemical protective suits the color of chocolate-chip camouflage. Their arms are locked around each other's waists. A few words underneath are written in firm ballpoint: *Nehi and Jake love the beach!* Sand spreads behind both soldiers as far as the camera lens can capture and for miles beyond.

Their 'beach' is the Persian Gulf, not Seaside Heights.

Nehi is still as skinny as she was back then, although lately the sharp, distinctive angle of her jaw has softened. Bash knows it's from whiskey and too much living.

Feeling useless as hell, Bash replaces the picture and moves the frame until it sits at the exact right alignment before he goes upstairs to face the mountain of clothes on his floor. He aligns the socks, matches them up and places them in the correct drawers. Underwear is folded lengthwise, and the t-shirts in his closet get tucked into neat rectangles before he piles them into rigid cotton bricks.

"She's sorry." London jingles into the room, sits on his bed, and tosses him the handcuffs. "Cried a couple times. Wants to talk."

Bash replaces the final stack of shirts and emerges. "I'll look in on her. Any chance Jake'll be back soon?"

"I texted him again." London waves her phone. "He had a VA workshop planned this week in Chicago, but he'll cancel."

Her declaration settles a new weight of worries on Bash's shoulders. How will he ever repay Jake and London? The debts he owes them are overwhelming.

"Bash." Her voice breaks into his private worries. "Did you tell her?"

"Tell who? What?"

London fixes him with her pale gaze. "You know who I mean. Julia."

"I will." He closes the closet and collapses next to her on the bed. "Just been busy lately."

Her fingernails are pink ovals. One pokes his side, and he grunts. "You better not wait. She'll get pissed if she finds out I came over tonight., not to mention that you're holding back a major part of your life from her."

He frowns, unsure. "Nah. Julia's strong. Plus." A yawn breaks through, and he thumbs his eye sockets. "She's got issues of her own." Exhaustion settles over him like an iron cloak, and he rakes his hair back.

"Julia, strong. Julia, issues. You're like a Neanderthal. You know that, right?"

London stands up to walk to the door. Bash catches her hand to pull her into a tight hug. "What would I do without you?"

"Be in jail, probably?" London breaks free, looks up into his face. "Okay," she adds, "I'm going. Get some sleep."

• • •

When he hears the tires of London's SUV spray the sanded driveway, Bash forces his eyes open. He could topple sideways and fall asleep on the floor, boots and all.

The old door sounds hollow under his knock. "Hey, baby." Nehi's voice is resonant – the way a classic movie star might greet a talk show host. She drags out the last word in each sentence and rolls it in her mouth, lovely as song. *Babyyyyyy.*

Bash takes the hand she holds out. "We can't keep on this way." The words are impossible to hold back.

She bursts into tears, releases his hand, and covers her eyes. Bash looks at his knuckles, the way they rest between his knees. On the linoleum there's a tiny brown stain. He'll scrub the floor again before he goes to bed and make sure the room is spotless.

His mother's sobs devolve to a litany of "I wish. I wish." After several hiccups, she adds, "Garbage truck." *Truuuuck.*

"Damn it." Bash feels his face tighten in frustration. He told the garbage company to reroute the truck months ago. They must have changed schedules again, not realizing that the loud truck would make her slip back into a PTSD event. "I'll call them again tomorrow."

"The windows were all blown out," she says. "We were able to look inside those rooms, into schools. Factories. Hospitals. Sometimes the rooms were painted red, except it wasn't red paint." *Painnnnnt.*

He strokes Nehi's hair. A soft touch sometimes brings her back from the Gulf and those red rooms. She's been through things he can never imagine, haunted by ghosts no séance can calm. After a while she stops crying. "I miss my daddy."

"You know I'll keep looking after you. Not gonna stop. But I hate having to trick you, hate using the cuffs. Hate all of it."

"I know, baby. I know." Nehi stretches and looks at the clock. "Why, it's past your bedtime!"

"We should both get some sleep. Right?"

Her grin is conspiratorial. "Don't want to get caught up past midnight." *Midniiiight.* Nehi winks, and Bash wonders how it's possible to love and admire and hate someone at the same time.

• • •

He knows he won't fall asleep right away. Bash waits until Nehi closes her eyes and starts to breathe evenly before he goes out to the barn to check on the pig. *Please don't let Nehi ever find her,* he thinks.

Harley is inside the cage, a little fur balloon that claws and wriggles when he picks her up. She settles quickly against his chest and wheeks hopefully for carrots.

Nehi's Vivitrol shot is scheduled for next week, and Bash considers cancelling the appointment. Maybe the damn stuff is doing more harm than good – it certainly didn't help her earlier. If he refuses the shot for his mother, though, it leaves them alone with nothing between Nehi and alcohol except his own fragile defense system.

Bash slumps against the wall of the barn and ruffles Harley's back, making her purr like a small motor. The sound is peaceful, and he's able to let go of his shadows for a moment. The sludgy shape of those fluids emerging from his mother's body, the handcuffs, the distress call to London – those things fade away.

In their place, he pictures an imaginary carved box made of walnut with splined miter joints and an inlaid brass hinge. Bash can nearly feel the ornate key, the smooth way it would slide into the lock. One day he'll make it for real.

Bash has a little mental hoard inside his mental box, saved for those nights when Nehi loses it. There's an A in a red circle on Julia's test paper, the blocks of folded clothes in his room, the carpentry tools his grandfather left him, the way Harley purrs under his thumb.

Now Bash can add the Little Free Library box. Soon it will be ready to be filled with Julia's books. Kids will come and look at the selection, choose a story to take home. Maybe Bash will find a book for Nehi and bring it to her.

And above all, there's red curls and a kiss in the tack room, sweet and brief – Bash's own private treasure.

CHAPTER 12.

Despite the late night, Julia wakes to the smell of fresh coffee. When she walks into the kitchen, her dad hands her a cup and kisses her cheek. Before she can say thanks for the coffee, he clears his throat. "I talked to a few people," he says. "Online. Found some groups on Google. Ever heard of it?"

"I've heard of Google." Julia hides her grin in the mug.

"The people are like me. You know, afraid of leaving the house. We talked about the outside. About a series of short-term goals." The skin beside his cheek is flecked with shaving cream, and it twitches as he speaks. "My long-term plan is to make it to your Little Free Library opening."

Julia looks up so quickly she nearly spills her coffee. "Yeah?"

He pulls her in for another hug. "Yeah," he says. "I'm really going to try."

There's rain outside, a good, clean sound. Julia gently disengages herself, picks up the toast he hands her by one corner, and sits at the table. Her backpack is slumped like a sulky toddler beside the door. Its contents include the completed presentation, a set of notes marked and memorized, a chemistry worksheet – also completed – and a sheaf of note cards in a rubber band. They're the start of Fry's final paper, but she hasn't been able to make them come together as one cohesive unit yet.

Mornings are usually a flurry of frantic hunts for a pen, a scrabble through a nest of papers, the cold realization she's left an assignment incomplete. "Julia's a classic underachiever," a guidance counselor once told her father on the phone. She listed Julia's grades, added a weary rant about how class rank would be vital in junior year.

Her father was never able to make it to the meeting they scheduled, and finally the overworked counselor stopped calling.

Today everything is organized and ready for class. She and Bash went through her papers the night before. He put everything into neat piles, made her get rid of more old notes. She'll go into class prepared to hand in the assignments. It's a peaceful thought, and the luxury of coffee by the watery window as she waits for Bash to show up is a nice benefit.

When his boxy Dodge Dart pulls into her driveway, she finishes the last corner of toast and chases it with coffee. "Ride's here," she announces.

Her dad looks up. "Do I need to meet this person?"

Naturally, he's picked the most inconvenient time to start parenting. She's about to say it's getting late when there's a knock at the front door, the one they never use.

Julia and her dad exchange an agonized glance. "Maybe if both of us pull really hard on the door?" she suggests.

"Come on," he says. "This could be a first step to get me to your opening." He pushes up the sleeves of his Rutgers sweatshirt, advances on the door in the foyer, and throttles the handle with a determined fist. The thing protests and squeaks, a dreadful sound like a pig led to slaughter.

"Give it up, Dad," Julia says. "This is entering teen embarrassment territory."

"Just one more..." He yanks the handle. There's a loud thump from the other side, and the door bursts open. Bash half-falls into the room, straightens, and brushes off his sleeve.

"Sorry," he says. "I could hear it was stuck. Knew one push in the center should do it." Julia hides her surprise as he holds out a palm to her dad. "Mr. Cameron? I'm Bash."

Julia's an expert at reading her dad's micro-expressions. Behind his elaborate nonchalance he's impressed. "The door's my fault," her father states. "I don't get out much."

Or at all, Julia thinks, but she doesn't say it. "Thanks for the coffee."

"Carpe diem," Dad says. "Um, could you maybe pick up some milk later?"

"Carpe diem," she agrees. "Sure, I'll get a couple of gallons."

The door closes behind her and Bash with another protest. "I'm going to fix that," he promises, "as soon as we're done with your box."

"You don't have to." Julia can't finish the thought, since he takes her into his arms from behind, threading his index fingers through her belt loops and hooks his chin over her shoulder. When she twists to look at him, black hair and brown skin, she can catch glimpses of sleep deprivation. Bash's eyes are rimmed with red, and his cheek looks as rumpled as a sheet after a rough night. "You okay?"

He nods but doesn't offer any details. He shepherds her to the car and opens the door for her with old-world courtesy, hardly the move she expected from a grumpy guy who does woodworking in the back of his barn.

As she gets in, Julia reflects the guys she's dated before him were more like hook-ups at parties. You got a text from someone, the boy gave you a time to meet, and later on you made out on an old couch with too much alcohol in your system.

Bash is altogether different.

Wanting to stretch out her legs, Julia pushes her backpack to one side and makes a hidden object clink under the seat. Bottles for recycling, maybe. Not beers, since he's told her he never drinks. She wipes rain off her palms on her jeans and watches the wet grass slide by her vision as they pull out onto the main streets. He drives in silence until they hit a stop sign, where with a sudden and violent motion he flicks up the turn signal and heads into a street lined with old trailers. Faded pinwheels and plastic daisies surround some of the small dwellings, most painted a defeated shade of blue. The wood sign on the corner proclaims they have just entered 'Heavenly Hills.'

Julia puffs her upper lip and frowns at Bash's profile. "Either you're planning to murder me here or you've got something on your mind." A brown square catches her eye, caught in the ancient carpeting, and she picks it up.

A piece of sandpaper, folded into the usual careful angles.

Bash's lips part, as though he has to suck in oxygen, and he holds out his hand. She gives him the sandpaper, and he rubs it against his chin. "The second one." Bash stares straight ahead, bare arms hugging the steering wheel, and he glares at the raindrops racing other down the windshield.

"I need to tell you a few things."

"Things," she repeats.

"Yeah." Bash turns, and she feels the pushpin of his intense stare on her face. "But I don't know what to say."

"Okay." Julia knows how he works. If she pries or begs, *come on, tell me,* he'll retreat like Harley when she's being shy. The only thing to do is wait it out.

The car rocks slightly from a gust of wind. An exasperated cry erupts from one of the trailers: "Sporty! Eat your damn breakfast!"

Bash whiffs a sound of soft surprise. "Do you think the poor kid is actually called Sporty?"

"Anything's possible," she laughs.

They sit in silence, and his smile dies away. He keeps himself wound so tightly, Julia realizes, pressed into his corner of the Dart.

"Did you ever not know where to start? I mean, because the story is so bad each part of it is worse than the other?"

"Yeah. Happens to me all the time."

"It's…" Bash scratches his jaw, scooches down in his seat, crosses one leg over the other, hurriedly sits up again.

"Don't hurt yourself." Julia's grin fades and she murmurs, "My dad hasn't left our house for the past year. It's why we couldn't open the door when you came to pick me up – he never goes out ever since my mom died. I have to open the windows and make him sit in sunlight so he gets vitamin D. And he makes soup every night. Potato, tomato, pea, chicken, mushroom – I've eaten every kind of soup there is in the world."

"How about shark's fin?"

Julia snorts and fake-punches his arm. She waits.

Bash's mouth frames his words before they actually emerge. "I have a secret," he whispers.

Around them, the crappy neighborhood seems to freeze as though it wants to hear what comes next. Julia sneaks a quick look at the way Bash's thick brows have V'ed into his usual frown.

"I won't tell anyone," she blurts.

He speaks at the same moment, his words blanketing hers. "I was the driver who crashed into your library box that night."

Julia flops against the car door, away from him. Her back hits the old-fashioned window crank of the dart, but she barely registers the pain. "What did you just – is this a joke? Some kind of sick joke?"

Bash's calloused fingertips flex on the vinyl driver's seat. "There were cops around the park when it happened. Maybe you heard the sirens? I just. Well. I couldn't let them see inside my car."

"Alcohol." Julia snaps open her seatbelt and reaches under the seat. The clinking object rolls into her palm, an empty bottle of bourbon. She yanks it out, hefts the cylinder like a club, and waves it under Bash's nose. "You had booze in the car, and you didn't want to get arrested for drunk driving. Right?"

"No, it's not…"

"You lied to me about not drinking. Because you felt guilty about it," Julia pursues. "Probably wanted to feel better about the whole 'ruining Julia's dreams and hard work' thing, so that's why you offered to build me a replacement."

"No!" Bash yells, although she's still talking. Their words tangle, a vicious knot. "It wasn't like that. I wanted to replace it, of course, just didn't know how to tell you."

Ghost shifts and leans forward between the two front seats, laying one finger on her pale lips, but Julia ignores the warning. "Didn't know how to tell me? And now you've figured it out?" She flicks her fingers against the sandpaper. "Oh, and you went back to the park. Tried to remove your paint from the sidewalk, sand it down so there was no evidence. Right?"

"How the hell did you – what?"

"I found the marks in the park, when Isaac and I…"

Bash slaps the steering wheel, the smack making her jump. "Isaac. Are you kidding me? I can't stand that guy."

"Yeah." Julia crimps her mouth so he can't tell she's about to cry. "Except he didn't sabotage my project, and you did."

"I can't believe you're like this right now, 0-100, straight to drama. I mean, 'dreams and hard work'? Really? It's a bookshelf, not a national monument." His eyes widen as though even he can't believe the thoughts spilling out of his mouth. "Julia," he adds. "I don't mean it that way. It's just that I just knew this would happen." Bash waves a hand between them, his explanation for the word 'this.'

She can't talk to him any longer, this beautiful boy who's already surging out of his seat, saying her name, reaching for her hand. To resist temptation, Julia springs out, slams the door in his face, and stumbles forward onto the cracked sidewalk.

Bash turns and rolls down his window, biceps bulging under his sleeve. "Could I please explain?"

"You should stay," Ghost suggests.

"I have to go." Spinning on one sneaker toe, Julia cuts across the mean little lawn of the mobile home where they parked, probably the one belonging to Sporty's family. Bash can't follow her there, not if she veers across the prickly landscaping into the backyard. She dodges an above ground pool scummy with pine needles and a dangerous-looking trampoline.

Julia reaches the end of Sporty's lawn and scrabbles over a rusty fence. A shout comes from the belly of the house – probably Sporty's dad wants her to stay off the grass. Right on cue, a second round of sulky raindrops starts to fall, sloughing off her hair and bared neck.

Duck your head, Julia thinks. *Make it out onto the next street. Hide behind…*

"A mailbox?" Ghost hisses. "He's out there, you know. Bet he's circling this neighborhood right now. Better idea – find your phone. There's only one person you can call, you know."

"I know." Julia's heart punches her ribs, and she digs in the back pocket of her jeans.

CHAPTER 12.

• • •

SUV's and jeeps swim like malformed sharks around the Buy the Way gas pumps. There's a red VW, followed by an old Triumph motorcycle. Its rider slumps, moody in the rain.

A sleek black vehicle pulls up in front of where Julia waits, shuffling her feet on the gum-spattered pavement. Its window rolls down, and a pale oval calls her name.

Isaac has arrived, a most unlikely angel.

Julia shakes rain out of her curls, climbs into the front seat, and gestures at the leather upholstery. She doesn't want to talk about what just happened. "Nice," she comments.

"Tiffany's car." Isaac props one arm along the back of her seat. "I kinda stole it."

"Never change," Julia sighs. "No, you know what? Ignore my bitchery. I'm in a shitty mood."

"No school today?"

"Yeah, there's school today, but. I just can't."

Isaac pumps one fist in the air. "Yessss. Okay, first we go shopping for stuff we don't need like incense and comic books. Next, lunch followed by a movie – I'm thinking horror is the way to go here – with overloaded popcorn and drinks the size of my head."

Ghost props both elbows on the console. "I like movies," she says. "I like popcorn." Her grin is bright in the darkened car.

Julia picks a hangnail. "I should go home. Even though I'm not in school, I should go through the books in my…"

"What?" Isaac asks.

"Damn it," Julia groans. "I suck. My backpack is still in his Dart. Can you believe it? I'm such an idiot."

"The Dart? Bash's car?" Fingers cupping her shoulder, Isaac pull her closer. "See, I knew it. Matter of fact, I picked up on a definite vibe between you two."

A sharp honk interrupts them. "Any day now," an irate driver shouts.

Julia pokes Isaac's ribs. "Maybe we should head out."

"Good call. Thing is, I got bored this morning? And smoked a few bong hits? So maybe you should drive?"

Still propped on the console, Ghost throws back her head and hoots with laughter. Isaac unbuckles his seatbelt and, without warning, climbs into Julia's lap. She exclaims, slides out from under his bony butt, and shimmies into the driver's seat.

There it's all too easy to turn, slump into his neck, and put her arms around him. "Is hugging you okay?" Julia pushes back and squints. "I didn't even ask. Sorry."

"Hey. I'm asexual, not inhuman." He frames her face with his hands so she has to tilt up her head to look at him, spiked hair and all. Raindrops slide down the dark glass windows, a liquid shield against the world. For the moment, she feels safe.

"My mom," Julia blurts. "She's not alive anymore. My dad won't admit it. He insists on keeping her room clean. Brings her meals – well, you know. Soup. I put pillows in the bed to make it look like she's still there."

"What? Julia, that's pretty weird shit."

"If I don't, he goes out of his mind and searches for hours. He kept me awake all night the first few nights it happened. Kept calling her name."

Isaac's palm is warm on her knee. He's murmuring something into her hair, but Julia ignores him. "She was killed instantly, you know? We had no idea until the damn hospital called."

She scrubs back her curls and fumbles in one pocket for a tissue. The call came, Julia reflects, in the middle of the night.

"And?" Isaac prompts.

"And – nothing. She bled out in the ambulance." After another prolonged beep from the annoyed driver behind them, Julia starts the car and pulls smoothly onto the two-lane road.

Bash is somewhere out there unless he's given up and gone to school. Maybe he's walking into Lit or Spanish with his squared-off homework papers. And how about her backpack? Has he left it in the Dart?

Isaac seems to read her thoughts. "I know Bash is a big dude, but if you need me to take a punch I'm good at it. Well, pretty okay at least."

"I don't need you to take a punch." Julia sucks in a long breath. "Let's not talk about him. And no movies, no mall, no popcorn – sorry. Come back to my house instead? Hang out while I figure out how to get my books back without losing my dignity?"

"No shopping or horror movie? Damn. Oh well. Okay."

• • •

She finds it's impossible to let go of Isaac, even when they arrive in her driveway. He walks her into the garage, opens the door, and closes it softly behind them.

"Julia. What are you…" Her father's voice dies out. "Who's this? Oh, Isaac. Right?"

He waves. "Hi. I gave Julia a ride home."

"Can you stay?" she asks.

"Yeah." He agrees without any shade of hesitation. "Just need to warn Tiffany about her car, but once she gets over threatening me with life imprisonment it should be fine."

"What about school?" her dad calls. "And who's Tiffany?"

Her mind searches for the quickest and nastiest way to shut him up. "What about your job? What about our mortgage?"

Dad seems to shrink. He closes his mouth and doesn't ask any more questions as she tows Isaac to her room. If her dad complains she'll leave the door open. Right now she *needs* Isaac to be there.

They sit pressed together, shoulder to ankle, on her carpet. Julia lets out a shuddering breath and turns to cry a little into his shoulder. She has no idea what she would have done without him.

"Phone," he says at last. "Tiffany."

"Sorry." Julia lets go and sits back. "What are you going to tell her?"

Isaac links his fingers behind his neck and stares at the ceiling. "Besides the schedule for this afternoon, which is hanging out with you,

I've been thinking about it for the past week. Might go to night school, learn something like how to code websites or design traffic patterns. I don't know."

Isaac's phone blasts suddenly, an incoming call. Julia waits while he answers and speaks in a low voice. She gets up and rustles the files about town permits on her desk so she won't overhear.

When he's done, he gets up and hands her the phone. "Tiffany sends her hugs and deepest prayers. Those were her words – hugs and deepest prayers."

Julia raises her eyebrows. She's never met the woman.

"And," he continues, "she invited you to come over this weekend so we can hang out, eat and drink, whatever you want. Can you?"

"No way. I have to get ready for the opening. I only have ten days left." A surge of anger sears her, and she twists away from him.

"I'll help you with anything you need." Isaac tugs her sleeve. "Look, it's your decision, but I just think – well, not that it's any of my business but you shouldn't stay all alone in your room all the time. Come and meet my mom. You and me, we're best friends, right?"

"I'll think about it." Julia recalls Dad's promise to make it out for her library launch. She sneaks a look at the screen of her own phones as a way to distract herself and stop thinking for a moment, but there are no messages. It's starting to piss her off – Bash has her backpack, after all, and she's going to need those assignments eventually.

Something scratches the wall, and Julia turns around. Her dad hovers there, awkwardly holding out two mugs. He clears his throat and looks at Julia. "Would either of you like some soup?"

CHAPTER 13.

Julia wakes to crusts on her eyelashes making everything rainbow. She blinks at the sound of water on her window, until it shuts off suddenly. *Hose*, she thinks, still lost in sleep. *Water from a hose, not more rain.* Dreams swirl around her, and she vaguely remembers her mom's appearance in a dream. It had been a nightmare about the two of them, Julia and her mom hunched together in the back of an old library. With dream logic, Julia knew they had to sort paperbacks and old classics, comics interspersed with heavy volumes of poetry all coming from huge piles of books that soared overhead and threatened to cascade over them.

There's a moment after waking up when Mom seems to have followed Julia out of her dream into the room, complete with her smiles and certainty that always kept their little family intact with unruffled good humor. Julia has a second to cover her face with the sheet before her sadness leaks through, tears sliding through her fingers as though they'll never stop. Her stomach contracts, and her joints ache from rolling into a tiny, miserable ball.

"I wasn't always good-humored," Ghost huffs. "Sometimes I could be a miserable bitch."

Julia's sobs stutter after another few blasts from the hose outside. *Who the hell is out there?* She glances at the clock and realizes it's already 11, far too late to make it into morning class. Somehow, she's ditched school for two days in a row.

She's about to get up to splash water on her face so she can talk to her dad without looking a complete mess, when her phone rings.

"Hello?" Her voice is a traitor, revealing the recent tears.

"Hey gorgeous. I hope I'm not disturbing you." Isaac's voice is husky, maybe from not enough sleep. She can't remember what time he finally left, but it was probably after midnight.

Julia sits up and covers her legs with the blankets as though the guy can see her over the airwaves. She's in bed wearing nothing more than an old t-shirt from her dad's college days. "Are you smoking a joint?"

On the other end of the line there's a long silence. "Maybe…" Isaac coughs and launches into a quick stream of words. "But don't hang up. Because I'm guessing you've ditched class again, and that is just so cool. Let's plan out that dinner at my house, which maybe should be a party and not just a meal. One last fling, is what I'm saying, before I start adulting and do stuff like take classes."

"I'm not hanging with you all day today." As if to prove a point, she forces her way out of the blankets and pads to her dresser for some clean clothes. A crumpled but clean t-shirt joins a pair of jeans on the floor before Julia remembers. "Crap," she mutters. "Bash still has my books."

"Yay! I mean, gosh darn it, what a shame." Isaac clicks his tongue and launches into a long, stoned giggle. "Now we *have* to do stuff together."

Julia picks up her clothes and a towel. A question blurts out of her before she can stop it. "Is there any chance in the world you would call Bash and get my books back for me? Ugh, no – forget I ever asked."

There's another long stream of air over the waves – more pot smoke, probably. "Yes! I'm all over it." Isaac's voice wobbles with excitement. "Are you kidding? I'll totally stake him out, figure out the situation, and get your textbooks back, like a quest."

Slumping on the bed, Julia realizes Isaac sees this as a video game. "No, I'll text him and figure it out." She hangs up without saying goodbye and stares at the clothes on her floor, spread-eagled like a limbless murder victim.

• • •

Showered and dressed, Julia goes to find her dad, but he's not in the kitchen or the living room. His desk is empty. Even his bedroom lies in shuttered silence. She's about to freak when the door from the garage opens and he peeks in. "Hey, kitten."

"Were you *outside?*"

"Yup."

"Whaaaat?" She can't hold back a wide grin.

He steps inside and toes off his old sneakers. "I was the lunatic with the hose. Hope I didn't wake you – I forgot how lawn stuff actually works." Already his skin is turning pink from unaccustomed sunlight.

"You were outside." She still can't believe it.

There's a stretched look around his mouth as he goes to the kitchen and hunts through the cupboards. "Figured it's time I took up some of the slack," he tells the coffee canister.

"Dad, this is so awesome."

"Um." Her father shovels grounds into their old percolator. "Are you planning to, uh… you know, school…" The lighted gas ring is a blue, deadly flower, and he sets the pot in the center of the petals.

Julia flops into her chair, not certain how she should feel. Life has always been cordoned into huge, indigestible chunks of work and school, running errands for her dad, and the library project. Her brain, with annoying precision, recalls several unfinished tasks. "Can I stay home today, just one last time? I'll make it to class tomorrow, I promise."

Their eyes meet, and his tongue flicks over his bottom lip. "Julia," her dad begins. "I'm hardly the person to give you advice. We both know that. But time spent inside grows like cancer, and all of a sudden you realize an entire chunk of your life has passed you by."

The cup warms her fingers. Julia blows on the coffee and remembers the past year like a series of snapshots. When other parents came to teachers' meetings and Back to School nights, her dad huddled in their messy little house. He missed the meeting with her counselor to help set up college applications. Julia played in a winter volleyball league, and Dad never made it to any of the games.

And at the hospital, Julia spent the final hours alone in the waiting lounge – a room filled with tweedy, uncomfortable chairs, all connected together like a metal spinal column.

There had been a basket of magazines on a glass table, and the top one showed a golf foursome in matching salmon sweaters. She still remembers their joyful expressions, the pink of their clothes bright against emerald grass.

Then her mom's funeral. An uncle showed up with a few distant cousins. Julia's dad never made it.

These memories flick through her brain. Julia pushes her chair away from the table so suddenly the coffee overflows her cup and spills onto the old, scarred tabletop, and finds her phone.

Sorry to bother you, she types. *I just really need my backpack.* Julia blinks and hits Send. Once it's gone, she decides to add another random thought: *It's in your car.*

Her dumb little messages bloop into blue ovals on her screen. Bash may be a drunken dumbass, she thinks, but he's hardly a thief. At some point he'll contact her about her stuff.

And the Little Free Library he built?

Julia's stomach contracts with panic. Bash has that as well, hostage in his barn. Should she ask him about it? Maybe call him? In her mind, she can hear her flailing to be civil to him after their argument. *"Hey, so I wondered if we can move forward, on the house at least. I mean the box. I mean the library. I can pay for your work if you wait a few weeks..."*

Just the thought of having that conversation makes her face burn.

• • •

Julia's skin feels too tight to sit inside their house. She finds a bottle of water, goes out to the garage, and slumps on one of the boxes of books. For a long while she sits in the hot and dusty enclosure, her own little version of hell.

"Everything will be okay. Remember? We solve equations one atom at a time." It's an empty echo, her memory of Mom's voice firm and clear in the smell of sunshine and old truck. Julia gets up abruptly, opens the box she's been sitting on, and picks up the book on top.

Of course, it's *A Change of Velocity.*

The book falls open easily when Julia pulls it out. "Are you really gonna read that again?" she once asked her mom, who laughed and turned the page. It had been winter, and snow rimmed the windows. Julia had pulled a chair into her mom's room so she could do homework.

Her dad had been there, she remembers. A silent figure, he dropped a kiss into his wife's hair.

Julia wishes she could relive that day. She wants to hear the rustle of the page as her mom turned to a new chapter, feel her own pencil scratching on composition paper, smell a chicken roasting in the oven. Julia places the book carefully in the box on the very top and closes the flaps.

Her mom is dead. Dead. Such a short, ugly word, with no room for interpretation or reincarnation. It is what it is, and she can't avoid it.

"Pissed at the world?"

Julia looks up and realizes a familiar black car idles in her driveway. Isaac leans perilously out of the window, his eyes rimmed with red as though he's been weeping blood. "Why are you here?" she demands.

"I'm going to get your backpack back, remember?"

"It's not here." Julia tilts her water bottle, chugs, and wipes her mouth off on one sleeve. "It's at Bash's place."

"Which I don't know where it is since he's Mr. Mysterious, so you need to come with me. Don't make that tragic face – you can hide under the seat while I negotiate the deal."

• • •

As usual, Isaac convinces her by wearing her out with his nonstop arguments. Finally, she agrees and climbs into the car, her stomach pitted with misgivings.

Isaac puts the car in reverse and pulls out into the street. "And don't forget dinner this weekend. Tiffany's super-excited to meet you, although I might have invited a few more friends."

"Oh no," she protests. "Are you kidding? I'm sorry, Isaac, but hanging out with a bunch of drunks is the very last thing I need right now."

"We won't do keg stands! Or shots! Or anything weird! Just a few beers."

"Drive," she repeats. Julia moves away from him and stares out at littered crumpled fast food bags and plastic bottles, the skins shed from travelers tossed onto the road. Who knows where they were driving? Maybe they were heading to a party or were late for a class. Maybe they were on their way to the funeral of an irreplaceable parent killed by some drunk, and they were so stricken with grief they forgot to throw their trash into garbage cans. "I don't want to be a loser. It's just that I also don't want to drink beers and do shots with people I don't know." A thought occurs to her and she adds, "Oh! And I might need to work. Sorry, but no dinner party this weekend."

"You're not on Aggie's schedule. She changed our shifts around."

"You were checking my schedule?" Julia frowns. "Why?"

Isaac launches into a long story about an iPhone alarm that didn't work, missing a shift, Aggie's threat to fire him. His eyes are crafty, darting in the dark interior of the plush car, and for a moment Julia panics. What is she doing in this space? How did she end up with this guy? She hardly knows him, even though he calls her his best friend.

But Isaac mutters *Sorry*, pats her knee, asks if she wants him to stop for different food or something healthy like a smoothie. After a few minutes of mindless banter interspersed with his usual jokes Julia feels soothed enough to sit back, watch the building swim past darkened glass.

The nail salons and pizza places grow more sporadic as Isaac heads deeper into the Pines, and Julia shuts her eyes. She remembers riding in her mom's car with her eyes shut against the sun so she could watch the orange kaleidoscope of tree branches and telephone poles against closed eyelids. She imagines what they're passing in Tiffany's car: maybe long stretch of farmland, abandoned houses, enclosed horse paddocks.

When she blinks herself to reality they're in a small lane fringed with scrubby trees. Isaac has pulled up to a gravel driveway, and it takes Julia a minute to recognize where they are. Bash's barn is a compass needle, centering the world so roads and trees wheel around her and shiver securely into place.

"I'm going to hide," she announces. "Seriously, just walk up and knock on the door and ask for my backpack. Nothing more than that."

"Yeah. I also want to look at your Library though. Haven't even seen it yet."

Her mouth falls open. "It's not in the house – no. No, Isaac. You can't. We are here for my books, and that's it."

"Shh, someone will hear you. I want to check it out."

She feels her fist tighten, nails biting into the palm. "You told me you would help, this is so embarrassing, you're such an asshole, I hate you so much."

Isaac's spiky head pokes forward, and he lands a smacking kiss on her cheek before Julia can dodge him. "I know. But I usually get what I want. And if it's not in the house, then…" He sniffs. "Sherlock Holmes deduces it is, therefore, in that barn over there."

Julia's stomach cramps, and her cheekbones twitch. It's not from fear, just the overriding suspicion Bash is a private person and any intrusion will be unwelcome.

"No worries. I'll be careful." Isaac opens his SUV door, jumps out, and closes it behind him with a posh, expensive click. Hands on his hips, he looks around him like an old-fashioned squire before heading to the barn.

Julia gets out after him and tries to head him off. "Isaac, this is the worst. We gotta at least call first! Bash and I aren't even talking right now."

"There are secrets here." Isaac's nose twitches, and he escapes her attempt to reel him back to Tiffany's SUV. "More mysteries from the mysterious Bash. I can smell them. Don't you want to investigate? Figure out this guy's secrets?"

"No, I really don't. Isaac, get back here!" She jabs one furious pointer finger at the driver's seat, but he disappears into the barn. His light hair is swallowed by the black mouth of the door leading to the stables.

The gravel slips under her sneakers as Julia slams back against the car seat. Finally, even though it's the last thing she wants, she gets out and follows Isaac, cursing under breath. Later she's going to let him have it.

Inside the barn, Isaac wanders past the stables, his hands trailing over the stall gates, and he looks like a perverse and serene angel in the shafts of dusty sunlight. Julia is so filled with fury it prickles in her veins.

"Hey jackass," she hisses with as much menace as she can muster. "Get your ass out of this barn, or I'm never going to talk to you again. Never."

"Never?" He turns and grins at her. "A bit harsh, don't you think?"

"Never." Julia folds her arms and raises one eyebrow. "Get back here. The last thing I need right now is your bullshit."

His face rocks as though she's hit him. "Bullshit. Wow. Harsh."

Harley chooses that moment to set up a loud wheek-wheek-wheek for hay, and he whips around. "Is there a guinea pig in here? I love piggies." Instantly he heads to the back of the barn and Harley's cage, where he falls on his knees. "Hey, piggy," Isaac croons. "Ooh, he needs water."

Julia reaches her side. "Harley's a female. Come on, you idiot." But Isaac is right – Harley's tube is dry.

"Water bottles. Car." Isaac leaps up and runs back to the outside, leaving Julia fuming silently.

He's such a jerk, she tells herself. *As soon as he gets back here and gives Harley some water, we're leaving. God, he's such a douche. God, what if Bash appears right now? God, please don't let him show up.*

Harley also needs food. Julia's mental list of insults continues to scroll in her brain as she fetches some hay and spreads it out in the little holder Bash has rigged up for the cage. By the time she's hooked the filled wire hay bin onto the bars, Isaac is back with a Fiji water bottle two-thirds full. "She wouldn't like a sub, right?" he asks, breathless. "I bought a few sandwiches for us, but probably carbs are bad for cavies."

"What's a cavy?" The sheer cheek of Isaac exhausts Julia.

"This guy. They're cavies, come from Peru originally. I wrote a report on them in 5th or 6th grade." The water glugs into Harley's container as

Isaac gabbles about his ancient project.

Julia breathes a silent prayer of relief when the cage is squared away. Harley pointedly turns her rounded furry bottom on them and eats hay, popcorning with excitement when a drop of water lands in her back. Isaac crows with laughter, and the pig darts into a tunnel Bash made out of reclaimed twigs from the pines around his barn.

"Okay. We're done." Julia stands, twists her hand in Isaac's collar, and hauls him to his feet.

"We did a good thing – admit it. Damn. What kind of person doesn't take care of their pet?" Isaac's still grinning, even as she frog-marches him past the empty stables. "Oh, hey – is this your little house? Sweet!"

He cranes his neck to look into the tack-room, but Julia pulls him against her side with an irritated yank. "No. You can see it in two weeks at the stupid opening in the stupid park, along with everyone else. Now get your ass out of this barn." She adds a shove to each word.

"Ow, that hurt," Isaac says in a mild tone.

They reach the entrance, where she peeks out to make certain no one's watching or yelling at them to get off the property. "Go, go, go," she urges.

As they huddle-run to the car, Isaac begins to splutter with laughter. When they're inside, his head collapses against the back of his seat. "That was awesome! Like playing Call of Duty, except for real."

"Just turn the key and drive," Julia orders between gritted teeth. She sucks in her breath as the motor starts up, but Tiffany's car barely makes a sound as they grate down the driveway and onto the road.

Isaac glides past the house, and the barn disappears in the rearview. Julia lets out her breath with a long Whoosh and collapses against the seat. "You suck. You suck so bad. I did not need to chase your skinny ass around a barn today."

"But you did." Isaac leans towards her, his face bright with determination. "Admit it, you forgot to be sad for ten minutes because you were so mad at me."

Julia feels her jaw drop. "Is this your version of therapy?"

"Maybe. Whaddya think?" Isaac doesn't wait for an answer. "Since we're best friends and all. *I know I suck.* Really, I do realize I'm a loser. And I'll go back for your books, I promise."

She leans against the door and regards him for a long moment. Through Isaac's window she can see the sky subside into gray and purple. Soon she'll have to get over to Aggie's Diner. "Wellll," she answers slowly. "You did make me forget how sad I was for a few minutes. So, there's that."

"So, there's that," he echoes softly before snapping his fingers. "Hey! I could buy you flowers for your opening. Roses, maybe. Ooh, sunflowers!"

"I don't want sunflowers."

"I want to buy you sunflowers!" His voice gets louder, and he bounces on the seat.

Julia expels a long sigh and tips her head back against his nonstop onslaught. "I don't want anything, not really. Okay, stop! Seriously, stop it. Donate to some hospital or something."

He relaxes against his seat, taps the steering wheel. "Maybe Aggie would let me put up a jar in the diner so we could collect for the fund. Tape a picture of your mom on there, like a In Memory Of sort of deal."

Julia jerks her head to look at his profile, hair teased into the usual spikes. "That idea actually isn't too horrible."

"I have my moments."

"Yeah, you do." It's time for her to get back, bike to work, figure out just how complicated life is going to be over the next two weeks.

Isaac drums his thumb and little finger against the dashboard, holding his hand in a Hang Ten. "Bash has a cool barn, right? And the house is amazing too. Unique, you know? Good place for a farm party. Not like my cookie cutter colonial."

"Or my split-level pile," Julia says absently.

"What's it like on the inside?"

"What?" She searches the Buy the Way bags and finds another Fiji water. "Bash's house? I've never been inside."

CHAPTER 13.

"What, never?" Isaac quits drumming, starts up the car, and reverses onto the road. He pulls a quick three-point in the old gas station's parking lot and heads back to Bash's driveway, running a commentary. "Come on. Julia, let go of my arm! It'll be fine. We have to check it out. He seriously never brought you inside the house where he lives and sleeps and breathes? I mean, who does that?"

"Isaac, stop it." Julia hits his arm, and the car swerves. "I'm serious – cut it out. Stop." She draws out the last word, but it's too late. He pulls up into a twist of overgrown wisteria behind Bash's Dart and hops out, jogs towards the house.

She emits a silent scream of frustration and rage before opening the door and following him. Maybe she can pull him back to the car and, if they do run into anyone, apologize for his behavior.

Who does Bash even live with? She's been too busy to ask.

Isaac's already halfway up the field in front of the house, dotted with the usual flutters of paper white butterflies. He runs bent over, hunched over as though he's about to puke on the wildflowers in Bash's lawn. As Julia calls his name in a strangled whisper, he hops right up the steps and lands on the neat porch surrounding the house. His hands cup the glass as he peers through, looking like an urchin from an old movie.

Before she can reach him he covers his mouth with one hand and backs away. Julia reaches the steps, and she beckons to Isaac with desperate strokes. It's like harnessing a hurricane or riding a tiger.

Isaac backs down the steps, half-falling onto her. Julia glances up to make certain no one has seen his ridiculous spy attempts and sees what has startled him.

The window frames the scene. A couple is embracing, the girl's long blond hair falling down her back. Her arms are around a dark boy, whose face is pressed into her neck.

Bash and London are far too intent on each other to notice Isaac.

Julia stumbles, nearly falls. Isaac's arm shoots out to catch her, and he's the one who drags her back to the wisteria, helps her into the car, and starts the engine. In silence they drive onto the road, heading back towards the world of supermarkets and diners.

Julia waits until they pass several minimarts and strip malls. "Well, that was fast, wasn't it? Nothing like finding a new girlfriend – and – and – he still has my backpack." Isaac opens his mouth, but her words continue to spill out like fish from a trawler's torn net. "And how am I going to get the Little Library?" Her neck hurts, and she rubs it. Isaac takes over the massage, driving one-handed. "Do you think he's been hanging out with her this whole time? While I worked at the diner and tried to keep my dad sane? Think they've been laughing at naïve Julia, so intent on building a dollhouse for other people's books while they made out and had sex together?"

"I don't know, honey," Isaac replies.

Julia slumps back in the seat. Forever the image of Bash and London will be burnt onto the inside of her eyelids, and there's nothing she can do about it. The weekend stretches before her, without school or books or work of friends.

"Hey, Isaac?" she says.

"What do you want, honey?"

"Tell your mom I'm coming over for dinner this weekend." She squeezes her eyes shut and hopes she won't cry.

CHAPTER 14.

At dinner, Julia's dad puts a plate in front of her, and she looks up from the chemistry website she's been trying to study instead of a textbook. "What's this?"

"Meatloaf." He turns back to the stove, hiding a grin.

"Meatloaf? You made meatloaf?" Julia hasn't eaten all day, and her rebellious stomach growls at the smell of potatoes and gravy. The food falls apart under her fork, but it's delicious, spiked with butter and parsley.

"Your mom's recipe." He brings his own plate to the table and sits opposite her. "How're you doing?"

She swallows some mashed potatoes. "Hanging in. I've got a plan."

He peppers his meatloaf and slides the shaker in her direction. "Heading back to school?"

"No." It's not what she meant to say but the thought of facing Bash and London again is just too overwhelming. "I'm not going back tomorrow. I'll stop by after classes are done and pick up my homework, figure out what tests I missed, which projects I need to start."

They eat in silence for a few minutes. Her dad seems to draw himself up, which always means he's got something on his mind. She waits for it, flinches when he says her name. "Julia, we need to talk."

Her phone rings suddenly, and she holds up a finger. One glance at the screen tells her it's Bash. The last thing she needs right now is to hear his excuses or lack of them. Maybe he'll try to talk to her as though nothing happened earlier between him and London, as though Julia's the village idiot or a dumb ragdoll on a shelf. She silences the phone and throws it into her backpack. "Go ahead. Sorry."

"It's okay." He frowns, his eyes turning into earnest, round blue marbles. "Was it one of your boyfriends?"

Julia laughs, a crack of sarcasm. "I don't have a boyfriend."

"No, but you do have a bunch of guys hanging around here lately trying to get your attention or pitch woo, or whatever it is nowadays.

Hook up? Is that the right phrase?"

She forks more food into her mouth and chews, staring at him. "It's certainly not pitching woo. And I don't want to talk about them right now."

"Staying home for a few days is fine. I'm the last person to tell you not to do it." He grimaces into his plate as he says it as though he's ashamed, and Julia reaches out to stop the flow of words. "I just – no, let me finish before I lose my courage. Staying inside can take over, get a grip in you so deeply you can't walk outside without wanting to throw up or fall on the ground, there's no way back except by fighting for every step. It's a constant war, like battling a tumor or your own addiction."

This admission, more than anything else during the entire long, disgusting day makes Julia break down. Her fork drops with a spray of mashed potatoes, and she covers her face with a napkin, feels her entire body shake.

A chair squeaks, and she finds herself pulled against her dad's thin chest, his words rumbling under her ear. "I *am* going to try to fight for you," he states. "And I know you've had to raise yourself for a long time, but I'm determined to see this through. I found a counselor who'll do sessions online and help me get outside, and not just to water the windows with the damn hose. I mean to make it to your opening, to the store, to the beach and one day – to a job."

Julia wipes her cheeks with the paper napkin and pushes away from his awkward embrace. There's a metal taste in her mouth, but she takes a deep breath. "How about the empty bedroom?"

He falls into his seat and stares at her. "What do you – can we not – I don't think I…"

"'Can we not?'" she repeats. "If not now, when? Dad, there's an empty bed in that room. Nobody sleeps there. You bring trays of food to a pile of pillows three times a day. Know what happens next?" Her father has one withered palm held up as if he wants to ward off her words like a malignant spell, but she presses forward. "I go in there. I find the disgusting congealed mess and flush your soup down the toilet or sneak it into the food disposal. One time you kept hovering over me, so I had to wait until you fell asleep to bury Mom's lunch outside, bowl and all. She's dead, Dad. I can't keep doing this. You have to accept the fact that she's gone. And…"

Her father backs away so swiftly his chair pitches backwards with a crash. Julia stands to block his exit. Under his breath he's muttering something, tumbled words laced with frightening, squealing breaths. He's trying to suck in enough air, Julia realizes, and for a moment she considers shutting up.

But they've arrived in this dark place after skating around it for so long. If she lets this go, their toxic mold will continue to feed off what's left of her tiny family.

"Dad." Julia pushes scalding tears off her cheeks with both hands and reaches for him. "It sucks, I get that, but we have to…" *confront this now or fall apart,* she wants to add, but it's too late.

With the same gentle touch he once used when she had fallen down and scraped both knees and elbows, Julia's father moves her out of the doorway. Appalled by what just happened between them, she doesn't move as his footsteps fade away.

There's no doubt about her father's destination. He's heading to the empty bedroom.

She doesn't drink beyond the occasional beer at a party, but Julia craves alcohol with sudden intensity. It's a want, no, a need to lose herself in an ethyl haze of rye or grain.

A bottle of brandy, left over from some long-ago holiday, sits beside the toaster. Julia imagines the pop of its cork, the way the liquid would glug into a glass, how it would burn her throat as she swallowed.

Julia goes to the high closet and gets down a mug, the first thing she finds. It nearly drops out of her grasp when someone knocks on the front door, a light and apologetic tap-tap-tap.

Unless Jehovah's Witnesses really have arrived, there's only one person who has knocked on that door. Her heart bounds, and she leaps out of the kitchen to wrestle with the handle. It takes a few tries and several bouts of cursing before she can open the entrance.

Her backpack sits on the top stop. As Julia cranes out of the door frame, she sees the Dart's blocky tail light pulse once, twice, three times to signal a right turn before disappearing into the night.

She breathes in the cool night air and hefts the backpack before closing the door and feeling for one of the stiff, uncomfortable chairs in the living room, a small space where no one ever sits down, and caresses the stiff zipper of her pack.

Ever since she bolted from the car, Julia has imagined her first confrontation with Bash. Her backpack has been a tiny thread connecting them. Now it's here inside her house, and he's gone with her silly little hopes. "I'm sorry," he might have said if he had just waited on the damn porch with his damn sorry self. "I should have told you earlier. we need to talk, come over to the barn and we can figure this out."

These are the words she's wanted to hear. Obviously, it's just not going to happen.

"How about my little house?" Ghost has appeared by the sink. "You still need to get it back from him, right? Bash, I mean. Not your father."

Maybe I should give up the whole idea. Julia hurts at the thought of quitting, an actual ache inside – as if her soul needed a root canal. She fills her mug with water, not brandy, and slurps it down.

"You can't give up now, not after you've done all that work." Idly, Ghost flicks at the water stream.

• • •

Waking up late is something Julia can definitely get used to. It's awesome to stretch and doze for another twenty minutes in sleep-warm blankets, at least until her mind clicks on and she has to get up and take the hottest shower possible to try and drive away the nightmares. Her dreams during the night were peaceful, for the most part – her mom was there again, sitting next to Julia with a huge smile on her face. "You're doing great," she had said.

The horror comes later from the memory of those words. They're so dreamlike, spinning out of Julia's mind. She hears them with her heart, not her ears, which is a dreadful betrayal. Mom's voice was so unique, the way she clipped off the final T with a tiny puff of air. Julia whispers the dream-sentence into the spray of hot water. *You're doing great.* Great-tuh.

Except Julia is not doing all that great. In the years to come those dreams will fade away, and she'll dream about someone silly like Isaac or D. Craniver, and how will she ever recapture that little decisive voice Julia loves so much? It's become a ghost.

It's become Ghost.

Tears, when they come, are colder than the scalding water. Her legs shake as she turns off the shower, towels off quickly, and drags on clothes.

The house is motionless as Julia drifts into the kitchen, lit by stripes of shivery light. There's no sign of her father. The kitchen chairs are empty, except for where Julia sits. It's occupied with her backpack, a squat reminder of real life.

When she picks up the percolator, it swirls with leftover coffee. Julia pours a cup and, after a moment's thought, the rest of the pot into another. Maybe her dad is in the next room. She could offer him caffeine as an attempt at civility.

Warmed up in the old microwave, the hot liquid smells like an old office. Julia drinks it anyway until the bitterness forces her to toss the rest down the drain.

"Dad?"

Her voice is swallowed in the morning quiet. Her father, if he's awake, doesn't answer.

Julia finds a few slices of bread, toasts them, and eats a few bites dry without butter or jelly. There's a withered apple in the crisper, and she peels it carefully. *When was the last time I took a multivitamin?* She rummages through the lazy susan, finds a bottle of lurid pills, and swallows one.

When she can't put it off any longer, Julia unzips the backpack. Her books wait inside, and Bash has added careful sticky notes inside each one. *Read pp. 125-153, study Chap. 14 for a test next Tuesday, use this section to fill out the study guide.*

In the silent kitchen, Julia leans her forehead on one fist and squeezes her eyes shut. After everything that has happened, Bash is still fixing things. First it was her Little Free Library dilemma, and now it's the mini-breakdown she seems to be going through.

His contact is still on her phone, right after Isaac. Julia hovers over the four letters, B-A-S-H, before powering down the screen. Class is going on, she tells herself, so she can't text him yet. Or call.

Not yet.

• • •

The chair in front of her desk is shaped to her body from years of use. Julia sorts her assignments in order of hardest to easiest, a trick Bash taught her in his barn when they worked together. Just because she's pissed off doesn't mean she's too proud to use his advice.

Most of the neighbors are at jobs or school, so the silence is broken only by the hum of the dishwasher and an angry jay outside. Julia smashes molecules on her chem paper so the equations balance equally and make some kind of sense – one atom at a time. As she plays god with the Periodic Table of Elements, she begins to see just how addictive silence can be.

Slowly and with a lot of erasing she works her way through the pile. When she looks up, finished with most of the assignments, the old clock radio says it's already past noon. Julia's stomach growls in agreement.

Lunch is leftover meatloaf. When she's finished and the dishes stacked in the sink, it occurs to her she hasn't seen her father all morning.

"Dad?"

Julia groans and pads down the hall to the old spare bedroom. "Dad?" she repeats.

No response.

With a long, inhaled breath, Julia opens the door of the room with the empty bed. It's still vacant, but the covers have been pulled off, as well as the sheets. Her dad must have used a lot of force – the mattress tilts off the box spring at an angle. The cupboard is open, and a pile of clothes spill onto the floor.

In the center of an octopus made out of old sweaters, an open book lies with its face folded primly to the bright wool. Julia knows what it is without reading the title: *A Change of Velocity*.

There is no response.

CHAPTER 15.

Isaac opens the door and does jazz hands when he sees Julia standing on the step. The contrasting cuffs of his shirtsleeves ride up his arms to reveal pale hair on tanned skin, making him look as expensive as Tiffany's car.

He pulls her in for a long hug. "I'm so excited," he mumbles into her ear. "I bet your mom's probably looking down from heaven right now, holding a glass of wine or tequila or whatever it is they drink up there."

Julia gets a mental flash of her mom in a recliner made of clouds, goblet in hand. "She'd make a great goddess," she murmurs and earns a bright smile in response.

"Exactly! Okay. Now." Isaac's tone becomes businesslike. "This party is small – tasteful. I only invited a few people. Not you-know-who," he adds.

"Oh." Julia waves as though she can sweep away the memory of what they saw in Bash's window. "Honestly, I'm fine. Got bigger things to think about. Real life issues." Julia has always sucked at drama. She'll definitely say the wrong thing when the time comes to get the Library box back from Bash.

Clasping her hand, Isaac tows Julia behind him into the kitchen. It's larger than she remembers from the first party. A group of kids stand around the island, one of them shuffling cards before dealing with short, practiced flips with two fingers. Next to him, a girl is mixing a tall pitcher of drinks.

Two of the guys wrestle over a huge bag of Doritos. When Isaac guides Julia to a spot next to them, she sees they're the Lacrosse Twins from Fry's class. "Lucky Charm!" one yells, flinging open his arms to engulf Julia in a huge hug. "Hey D-Bag, it's our Lucky Charm!"

"I got eyes, Butthead" D-Bag says around a mouthful of chips.

"Hi, guys." Julia disentangles herself from Butthead's embrace.

The girl at the island spins on high-heeled sandals and offers a drink to the card dealer. "Virgin daquiris, Isaac," she announces. "You don't have to pour alcohol down your throats, you know." Julia realizes she's not a girl at all but an older woman, stunning in simple white shirt and slim jeans. "Are you Julia?" she asks, handing out a stack of miniature Solo cups. "Oh. My. God. I'm so excited to meet you. Tiffany," she adds.

"Don't start," Isaac warns.

"Oh, shut up, you." Tiffany puts down the pitcher and beckons to Julia. "Ignore my son. Can I talk to you alone for a second? Go ahead and give everyone a drink, Ize," she adds. "I'll bring her back in one second."

Julia releases the edge of the island and ignores the lamentations from the Lacrosse Twins. "Lucky Charm! Come back!" Butthead shouts.

Tiffany tells him to stop and struts across the hardwood floor to a small, octagonal space off the kitchen. "It's supposed to be a dessert room," she explains as Julia looks around. "Major bump-out upgrade, so of course my husband had to get it when we built the house. We never actually eat dessert in here, though." She sits on a padded bench, pats the seat next to her, and clasps Julia's hand. "I'm so sorry about your mom. Ize told me all about it." Her eyes are huge and darkly sincere, a lovely contrast to the lion streaks in her chestnut hair.

"Thank you," Julia mumbles, since Tiffany seems to expect something.

"No." Tiffany moves their joined hands up and down as though it's the only way to convey the depth of her emotion. "No, thank *you*. I can't tell you what you've done for Isaac. God knows I love that boy, but he drives me crazy! And you got him a job, and he's actually going to work which is just such a miracle."

"He's a good guy."

"He is! And so few people see that in him." Tiffany moves closer. "And I have to tell you something else. I'm part of this Facebook group, and we pray for people? Who have passed on? And let me just say when an angel passes, we see rainbows *everywhere*. It means they've gone to heaven."

"Okay." Julia has no idea where this is going.

"Well. I saw a triple rainbow yesterday!" Tiffany fixes Julia with the brown pushpins of her gaze. "Took a picture on my phone and posted it to the group myself. Yes, I did. And I just know that your mother is in heaven right now, and she's looking over us." She lets go of Julia's hands, makes the sign of the cross, and kisses her fingertips.

The depth of Tiffany's manufactured sincerity touches Julia. It's obvious the woman is offering Julia the very best she has with her Facebook rainbows and angels. "Thanks." She wishes she had more to say.

The word appears to please Tiffany, and she pulls Julia in for a hug against the hard cones of her bra. "I lost my uncle when I was in high school. Daniel, his name was? Never forgot him. He was a gift from God we just weren't allowed to keep for too long."

Her simple belief stabs Julia in the corners of her eyes, makes the dessert room slide sideways in watery crimson and gold. "Oh, God." Tiffany reaches over, plucks three Kleenexes in quick succession from a leather tissue box holder, and hands them to Julia. "Here I am making your mascara run."

"I don't wear mascara." Julia smiles weakly.

"Well, you should. You are gorgeous. Gorgeous," Tiffany repeats, holding up a palm for emphasis. "A little make-up, some new clothes, you'd have a string of guys shooting each other for your number."

"Lucky Charm!" Butthead bellows from the kitchen. "We need you!"

"There," Tiffany whispers. "See? I told you."

• • •

When Julia returns to the kitchen, the daquiri Isaac gives her is fruity and so sweet it curls her tongue. "Shh," he whispers. "We'll spike them when Tiffany goes upstairs."

She takes another sip and shakes her head. "Can I just get a beer or something?"

Instantly the Lacrosse Twins look at each other. "Yeah," D-Bag says with satisfaction. "A girl after my own heart."

"Don't you dare drink and drive!" Tiffany shouts from the depths of the refrigerator. "Ize, you know the rules. Now, I'll just put out more food and disappear from your lives." She emerges with trays of sliced subs, vegetable platters, fruit, cookies, and a huge tiramisu.

"Marry me." Butthead wraps his arm around Tiffany's shoulder.

She dodges his kiss with expert precision. "Oh, no, don't start. Get off me. Now, you kids clean up your mess. Bottles in the bucket, trash in the garbage, and I don't want full cups all over the house tomorrow spreading germs or whatever. Wipes and bleach are under the sink, more paper towels in the pantry. You hear me, Ize?"

"I hear you."

Satisfied, Tiffany leaves the room. A second later she yells, "I'm catching up on my shows upstairs, so if a neighbor calls the cops I'll be really pissed off!"

• • •

They play Cards Against Humanity, even though Julia's never seen the game before. "It's easy," Isaac states. "You just have to know your judge." After a few rounds Julia picks up on the winning strategy. The most perverted cards always win the point, especially if D-Bag or Butthead are judging.

She reaches five points first, and Isaac pours some daquiris to celebrate. Julia sticks to beer, but she still feels loose, easy. It's a fake sense of calm, and she'll pay in the morning. Still, it's worth it not to have to think about her parents for five minutes. It's also nice not to remember Bash and London in each other's arms.

Isaac gets bored with the game and gets out some dice marked LRC. "We all need three bucks," he states. "Wait, here. I've got singles." Already he's handing out money, pulled from a drawer in the kitchen.

"I don't want your money," Julia protests, but the bills are thrust into her hands.

"Someone get Julia another beer so she'll get over herself." Isaac grins and rolls the dice, has to take a shot when one falls off the table. Butthead calls it the Helen Keller rule.

"Really?" Julia mumbles. "How about the Wilma Rudolph rule?"

"Who the hell is Wilma Rudolph?" D-bag asks.

She looks up, horrified to see everyone around the table looking at her. "Oh. Uh, she was a famous Olympic runner. Won three medals in Rome."

"Never heard of her." The girl who promised Tiffany to clean up holds out her cup for another drink.

"If *only* we had access to a universal source of instant information." Isaac raises one eyebrow, clicks his tongue, and pats the smart phone in front of him. "Hey, look here – Wilma Rudolph. American runner in the Olympics."

"Cool." The girl nods, sips. "What's the rule? We have to throw the dice fast or something?"

"Yeah." D-Bag leaps up with enthusiasm. "You've got ten seconds to shake the dice and figure out where your dollars go or you have to drink. Or chug." He gestures at Julia's beer with his own bottle. When he flings the dice at the table, one plunks onto the ground.

"Helen Keller," Isaac crows. "That's a rule too."

"Why do we come over here all the time again?" D-Bag turns to Butthead.

"Because his mom is hot, and she puts out lots of food."

"Oh. Yeah. I forgot."

• • •

By the time Isaac gets hungry and opens the tray of subs, Julia has won several games and holds two pockets filled with dollar bills. She tries to sneak them back into his hands, but he scowls and threatens her with a plastic spoon. "No way. You were the winner."

She accepts a paper plate loaded with food. The beers have made her hungry for the first time in three days, and she devours a sandwich with chips. D-Bag sits with his feet up on the windowsill, a girl on his lap. Isaac and Butthead flank Julia's chair, trying to out-insult the other. In the background music with a heavy backbeat plays on a hidden speaker.

"Okay." Isaac stands suddenly, spilling a wave of beer onto the hardwood floor. "We need to go outside."

"Why?" D-Bag frowns and waves at the luxurious kitchen. "I'm fine here, no problems."

"We need to go outside," Isaac repeats with drunken insistence.

The girl jumps off D-Bag's lap, and the partiers troop through the kitchen to a pair of wide French doors. Isaac opens them, and the outside lights up to reveal a stone patio loaded with wide umbrellas, marble urns, several potted plants, and a wall fountain of a lion spitting a constant stream of water.

Isaac ignores the trickling water and plummets down a rounded set of stairs to the lawn. He waves, and Julia joins the others around him as he holds up his drink. "Now, there's someone who can't be here with us tonight," he states. "So, this is for Julia's mom."

He pours a healthy dollop of daquiri onto the grass, and D-Bag echoes him. "For Julia's mom."

Julia watches as the others solemnly pour pink cocktails and cold beer into Tiffany's fancy landscaping. She's not the only one affected by what happened. D'Bag's girl never knew Julia's mother, and maybe it doesn't matter.

She pours out her beer and, as though following a silent signal, everyone surrounds her so she's inside a warm little cave comprised of arms and beer breath. It's pretty gross.

It's also nice, one of the best things to happen since the split with Bash.

CHAPTER 16.

"Julia. Get up," Mom insists. "Wake up. It's time."

"Stop knocking on the lid," Julia slurs. "Someone's going to hear and make me get out, and I want to stay here longer with you."

In the dream she's lying next to her mother inside a coffin, but it's not a scene from a horror movie. Instead, Julia finds it comforting to hide away from the world in secret, padded darkness.

"Julia," Mom repeats, except it's not her mother who's talking. Dad stands in the frame of Julia's door, shadowed by a tall splotch of brown in the hall.

She sits up and pushes at the spirals of hair stuck to her cheekbone. "What? What is it?"

Her dad jerks his head in the direction of the smudge standing behind him in the hallway. "I hate to wake you, but your suitor is here. He says you two need to talk."

Julia sits up. She's still in the jeans and t-shirt she wore to Isaac's party. A cold wave of rage rushes through her veins at being woken up so suddenly – and by Bash of all people.

"Suitor." Julia snorts. "I'm going to shower. He can wait until I'm dressed. This sucks, as a matter of fact." She refuses to look at the two males in the hall as she gets up, shoos her father out, and slams the door in their faces. A thought occurs to her, and she opens it to add, "Go away."

Her clothes in the closet won't cooperate, slipping out of her clumsy fingers and making her curse. She needs coffee and breakfast food with high fat content, not a surprise morning visit.

Armed with clean clothes and a towel, she stalks to the bathroom and showers as aggressively as possible. It's tempting to marinate in the hot water for hours, but their small water heater is old and sluggish. After a few minutes the spray runs cold, and Julia tumbles out to dry off and get dressed. She brushes her teeth, makes certain she hasn't left a brushstroke of toothpaste foam on her cheek. There are purple thumbprints of exhaustion under her eyes, but she's too angry to worry about something as mundane as makeup.

• • •

Her father's back has an apologetic slant as he hunches over his computer. Across the room, Bash stares out the kitchen window into the scrubby front lawn. Julia can almost see smoke rising from his nostrils, dragon-style. She stalks between them to lean against the Formica counter and crosses her arms, waiting for someone else to make a move.

Bash's heavy eyebrows descend when he turns to face her. "Sounds like you had a good night last night," he states.

"Looks like you had an even better day on Thursday." Julia turns to the percolator, but it's empty. When she goes to dump the old filter, Bash is right behind her, so close they nearly touch from toe to chest. The infinitesimal distance between them shivers with atoms, molecules, and unbalanced equations.

"What the hell are you talking about?"

"Ask London." Julia shoves the percolator into the sink. "She was there."

He blinks. "Damn," he says. "Were you...?"

They stare at each other in the old kitchen. Julia smells chicken and onions, so her dad must have gone back to his soup habit.

"Let's go outside. Please." Bash tacks it on as though he's just remembered the word.

Julia pushes away from the counter and heads to the garage. She beckons for him to follow with a quick, angry jerk of her head.

Bash steps out into the small, hot space next to her truck. It's not nearly as peaceful as her mom's dream coffin. "Those steps are going to fall apart," he declares. "Nail's nearly out on the bottom. Wood rot. See?"

"I don't care about the damn steps." Julia turns away so suddenly it makes her nearly black out, and she staggers. When he steadies her with an arm, she pushes him off and marches to the ungainly maple tree dropping miniature, green helicopters all over the driveway.

"Okay." Bash approaches, his palms lifted in supplication. "Obviously you're still pissed off at me, even though you still haven't given me a chance to explain."

"And it's also obvious you're mad at me for going to a party last night. Since we're on the subject." The shade under the maple tree is cool, but there's a promise of heat in the late morning. Julia skewers him with his gaze and shoves her hands in her back pockets, wishing she had worn shorts.

He folds his arms over his strong chest and tilts up his chin. "What do you expect when the girl I'm talking to takes off with some other dude and doesn't answer my calls?"

"Isaac is a friend, not that I have to explain myself."

"You're mad at me because of a bottle in my car, so you head off to drink at parties now? A little hypocritical, don't you think?"

Julia sucks in her breath and wheels to face the maple. There's a little bunch of seeds dangling by the trunk, and she picks at them, snaps one in half.

Bash huffs out her name. "Julia. Jesus, what's even happening here? I didn't mean to say that."

"The people there were really nice," she says to the seeds in her hand. "We talked about my mom and poured – I know it sounds stupid. We poured beer on the grass for her."

"You were drinking?" He's right behind her again, setting molecular chains in fluttering motion.

The world whirls as she spins and pushes his hard body with the jittery strength she has left. "This is nothing to do with you." Julia swallows, uncomfortably aware her stomach is churning from too much alcohol and not enough food or sleep. "Not after you and London had your little love scene."

"What?" His eyes narrow, the dark V rises in what seems like genuine confusion. "I have no idea what you're talking about."

"At your house." As soon as the words are out of her mouth Julia remembers she's given herself away.

His face darts closer to hers. "Were you spying on me?"

"I, uh." It's her turn to search for the right words – which, of course, don't exist. "Isaac wanted to see the Library box. Before I knew it, he'd taken us to your barn. I told him to cut it out, but he snuck up to your house…"

Bash sticks one hand in his hair and turns away from her. "Again with this guy. Are you kidding me? You and this asshole looked in through my window – what, to check up on me?" He frames the final word with air quotes. "I don't need this bullshit."

Julia shakes her head. "I don't need someone who helps me out just to feel better and hangs out with other chicks."

He makes a disgusted sound in his throat. "I've known London and her family for years. You don't know what you're talking about – but I don't have time to explain it to you. This…" One square-tipped index fingers points at his chest and hers. "Well. I guess it's good we found out now before things got really crazy."

"I guess it is."

Julia refuses to watch him drive away. She walks into the garage, pulls down the door, and waits until she hears the Dart starts up and heads down the street. When the engine dies out into the distance she slumps on a carton of books and sobs so violently she feels sick.

• • •

Staying home is impossible since she'll only curl up in her bed and talk to Ghost. Even after her disastrous and recent life choices, Julia knows that's a bad idea.

A call to Isaac is not happening. His gossip and lack of attention would drive her out of her skull.

Julia freshens up, washes her face and brushes out her hair. The dollar bills she won the night before are all over her sheets, shed like green snake skins during the night. Julia picks them up, sorts them into an untidy stack, and shoves it into her back pocket. She mumbles a few words to her dad's back and gets on the bike, heads over to the diner.

By the time she arrives her stomach is curling in on itself with hunger. Aggie takes one look when Julia walks through the door, sets down the coffee pot, and pulls her in for a long hug. "Oh, honey," she says.

The wad of bills is heavy in Julia's hand. "I really need to eat something," she says. "Do you think Ben would scramble a few eggs for me?"

Aggie waves the money away. "You kidding? I'm buying you the biggest, greasiest breakfast on the menu. No, don't you dare wave those nasty bills in my face. Just so happens serving lots of calories is something I *can* do." The volume of her voice soars to airplane takeoff level. "You hear that, Ben? Plenty of skid grease, wreck 'em on a raft. A real biscuit grabber."

"I heard." Ben's voice is muffled by the clatter of spatulas and spoons in the back. "Tell Julia whoever it is I'll kick his ass."

"Ben's gonna kick his ass," Aggie repeats like she's the only one who can understand her ex-husband. She pats a counter seat and peers at Julia's face. "Who is it? Better not be Isaac. I'll drag him behind the dumpster by his little blond curls and let him have it."

"Gonna have to beat me to it," Ben hollers.

Julia feels her face defrost for the first time since she was yanked out of the wonderful dream about her mom's coffin. "No, Isaac's fine." She picks up the coffee Aggie pours for her and takes a long sip.

Reenie rounds the corner with three plates of pancakes up one arm. "It's probably that other guy," she says. "The gorgeous one with black hair and angry eyes, looks like the cover of a romance novel."

Aggie wordlessly hands Julia a huge cinnamon bun. "Yeah, it's him. Right? I'm always right."

The pastry is warm and flaky on Julia's tongue. Without looking, Aggie pulls a plate the size of a hubcap off the serving ledge and puts it by Julia's elbow. It's loaded with fried potatoes, scrambled eggs, French toast, and a woodpile of bacon under curled steam and melted butter.

"You're getting too skinny," Reenie expertly juggles a tray loaded with dishes and pokes Julia's hip. "See? You're all bones."

Her hangover makes her so hungry she barely tastes the food. Julia shovels it into her mouth, then spies the schedule for her week of shifts. All the squares with her name have been changed to Isaac, and she points to the paper in its plastic sleeve. "What's up with this?"

Aggie appears with a flat of eggs and hands them to Ben. "You've been working too hard. Relax, concentrate on yourself for once. We'll put you back on as soon as you're ready – don't you worry about that. Now finish your food."

• • •

The bag with her leftover breakfast is heavy with added treats – wheels of cookies, pyramids of cake. Julia leans on the refrigerator and stares at the white bag nestled between glass jars of soup in the refrigerator.

Anger has shaken her out of her usual entropy. She's spent over a year catering to her father's fantasy, and why?

"Time to sit down and figure out the answer to that problem, Julia," Ghost says.

I don't want to make him see how empty Mom's bedroom is. I'm afraid of what might happen if I make him confront the truth, Julia thinks.

Silence, like layers of dirt packed over a grave, has made both Julia and her dad complacent *and* complicit to living a lie – which is no life at all.

But what about Ghost? What about that?

Julia makes a sudden decision and goes to the corner cupboard. The plates clatter as she gets one down, slams the door shut, and opens the bag from the diner. Julia reaches withdraws a slice of chocolate cake, puts it on the saucer, and stabs it with a fork before marching out of the kitchen to deposit the treat next to her dad's computer. With one foot, Julia feels for the other chair and drags it forward so she can sit next to him.

"I remember her too, Dad." She knows she doesn't need to say any more.

He thumbs a button on his sweater, tracing its chipped surface with a broken nail. "When I met her, all those years ago on my first sales trip, I couldn't believe someone so bright and beautiful would even look at me. But she did. When she… when it all happened, I hid out and let you deal with everything."

Julia has tried to forget the confused burble of lawyers' phone calls and hospital forms. "What are you saying?" she asks.

"I meant it when I said I wanted to attend your opening."

Shit, the opening. "Ah, yeah. I still have to work on that or it might not happen."

Dad doesn't move. "Does that boy have anything to do with it not happening?"

She can't hold back a laugh. "Yes, he has the library box in his barn. And, no, we're not speaking right now. So."

His eyes are doing that thing where they melt at the corners as he starts in on a speech about how it's Bash's loss. Perhaps he's rehearsed in his head at night when he lies in bed unable to sleep.

• • •

Julia escapes to her room where she scowls at the backpack. The chemistry essay is the last thing she wants to think about.

When she unzips it, Spanish, history, and chemistry books are wedged together. Julia pulls them onto her desk, sighs as she opens the thick pile of papers clipped together with notes from her teachers. *Quiz Monday. Pgs. 135-159, answer all questions in review sections. Begin class presentation.* And, of course, in Mr. Fry's neat italic writing, a note to continue her final essay for class.

She feels in the bottom of the bag for a pen, and her gut clenches on fried potatoes and scrambled eggs. There's a square of folded paper lurking under the books, the one she avoided reading the day before.

Here are the things I miss about you, Bash has printed in his neat, inked capitals.

1. Your laugh.

2. Your hair.

3. The way you always know what I mean.

4. Your soft words when you first saw what I built for you.

*5. The way you frown and bite your lip when I show you
how to sand a piece of wood.*

6. Your concentration face.

7. Julia. I miss everything. I miss you so much.

It's been sitting in the backpack for several days. She knows the words no longer belong to her, and the feelings he's written have expired. The paper crumples in Julia's fist, but she can't quite summon the energy to throw it away.

"It's your first love letter, after all," Ghost points out.

With her elbow, Julia smoothes out the crumpled sheet. She hides the note under a pile of novels on the corner of her desk before diving into the cold waters of chemistry homework.

CHAPTER 17.

Bash watches Julia as enters the chem lab. She plops into a new seat in the corner, far from Bash's table.

"Guess we're allowed to pick new seats." London stands, picks up her purse, and with a look of triumph sits next to Bash.

Bash knows exactly why Julia has moved, but it doesn't make things any better. He also knows he's wearing his usual frown. It's gotten him into trouble in the past. "You just looked guilty," one teacher apologized when it turned out Bash wasn't the one cheating on a test. Apparently, he has Resting Criminal Face.

Julia sits next to the chipmunk girl who exclaims over everything. He can already hear her chirps from across the room.

"That's so awesome! Love it! You're amazing!"

Julia's going to hate sitting next to Chipmunk Girl – she's far too calm for that kind of noise. Even the fight they had with in her scrappy front yard was quiet. In fact, he wishes she had yelled at him instead of picking seeds and whispering about Isaac. Maybe if she lost her temper, the heat could finally break the ice wrapped around his bones.

"Bash," London hisses.

He shakes his head, willing himself to wake up. The past few days have been a horror movie, its intensity multiplied by jump scares and panic: brown streaked shit on white paint, pointless calls to the VA, Nehi's hoarse screams in the night as she wakes up and vomits out another huge mess for him to clean. He's scrubbed the floors and walls in her bedroom for hours, and the stains still won't come out.

Maybe he'll try ammonia tonight, since the bleach is doing squat.

London has told him the VA will send a new counselor. The last one was a disaster, but he has no other choice. At least if someone comes to sit with Nehi, Bash can get his homegrown systems back in order: bucket refilled with rags and cleanser, sheets washed and changed, house purged of alcohol.

Where the hell is she stashing it, anyway?

He's so exhausted he can't think straight. Sponges, mops, and laundry don't leave much time for homework or sleep.

As usual London is right there for him in class, providing answers and nudging him when his head nods with exhaustion. Jake's due back in town in a few days, so Nehi will also have some real support instead of the ragged care Bash gives her.

He wants to erase the past few days from his memory. But more than anything he wants to watch Julia, the way her careless curls bounce as she responds to Chipmunk Girl's answers.

The only thing he doesn't like is her friendship with Isaac, the guy who holds wild parties in a huge house. Bash simply can't have more liquor in his life, not after the rank odor of Nehi's fluids over the past few days. The thought of drinking beer or doing shots makes him gag.

Bash swipes his face with one hand and remembers the stacks of shirts and pants in his closet, the neat piles reorganized until the corners are exact. The squares of homework papers. How he had to mop the floor until his back nearly gave out. That list he wrote for Julia and hid in her backpack.

What the hell is wrong with me?

Mentally he adds to that list: *How your lashes rose and fell when you watched me sketch out your house. Your soft words when you held Harley and murmured to the pig as you held out a bunch of parsley...*

Jesus. Harley. The thought of the little animal makes his heart stutter. With everything going on, Bash hasn't had a minute to visit the barn and feed the guinea pig. Harley is sitting in a pen without food or water.

He sucks. He sucks as a human being.

Bash stands so suddenly his chair topples over with a loud bang. "What are you doing?" London demands just as the bell rings. Not bothering to answer her, he tears out of the classroom past groups of students who flood the hall with hoots of chatter.

In the student parking lot there's a cold scrim of mud like a dark mouth sucking at his heavy boots. Bash runs to the Dart, guns the engine and drives. He buckles the seatbelt as he backs away from the school and heads towards the barn and Harley.

Of course, there's a ton of traffic. He tries not to slap the wheel or give anyone the finger. Still, Bash curses out each red light, every slow pedestrian. Sweat prickles under his collar, and he keeps chewing one corner of his lip. The short drive seems to take fifty years.

Finally, finally he reaches the graveled driveway.

The wheels screech as he brakes and runs out of the car, through the sanded pines and into the barn. "Harley," he calls. "Sorry, piggy. Sorry, sorry, sorry." If he says it enough, maybe she won't...

The guinea pig wheeks as soon as he enters her stall, and Bash falls against the divider with relief. Her water is low and she's definitely hungry, but she's alive. He scoops her up and finds a bag of dried apple snacks, watches her eat one with determined munches. "I'm a disaster," he tells her. "You really don't deserve this, do you? You don't ask for anything besides a spare lettuce leaf now and then."

Harley pours out of his hands with an aggrieved huff into her spare box. Then Bash fetches fresh liner and shovels out the soiled hay in her cage. He lines the bottom with old towels, pale with repeated trips through his grandfather's decrepit washing machine, and covers them with the new hay. All the old stuff goes in a bag for the compost pile behind the house.

After a trip to the kitchen to clean and refill Harley's water bottle, Bash sees the tack-room where he stores his tools. The door stands propped open, not closed. He knows he always clicks the door shut when he leaves the barn.

Isaac. The guy must have left it open when he and Julia snuck into the place. Bash closes his eyes for a second and feels his lungs inflate with rage. He can imagine what it would feel like punch Isaac right in the middle of his wide, toothy, irresponsible smirk.

Breath whistling in his throat, Bash enters the tack room. Everything is just where he left it. Julia's house stands on the bench, all tools are stashed away, and the closet door on its hanging hinges is closed.

What if Isaac looked inside? What if he touched the diamond partition box?

Bash slides back the door and winces at the squeak the hinges make. He'll have to oil them later after he's given Harley more treats as a reward for surviving, and he goes to replace her water and pick her up carefully out of the spare box. As though she reads his mind, the pig wheeks and clicks her teeth, always ready for food.

"Snacks? You want snacks? Of course, you want snacks. We'll go inside for some carrots right now..." Bash's voice dies out. One of the boxes on the bottom row has a thumbprint on it. He keeps the wood dusted and polished, as clean as the day his grandfather made it, and the print stands out against that gleaming finish.

Seriously, he's going to find Isaac and pummel him until that rich kid never wants to approach Bash's barn again.

Bash takes the keyring down from its nail up on the wall. Juggling Harley in one crooked elbow, he finds the right key (brass with three teeth) and fits it into the lock.

The diamond partitions are still filled with drill bits, but a yeasty, chemical smell hits him as soon as he opens the lid. Harley scrambles up into his neck and snuffles into his collar.

"It's too heavy," Bash tells her. "Something's wrong." Carefully he grasps the partitions by the widest angles and pulls. The entire section comes out, revealing a secret drawer he never knew was there.

Three bottles tilt against the velvet side of the box, two filled with a brown liquid. The third is clear, the cheapest brand of vodka available.

Bash has finally found Nehi's stash.

With a final apology to the guinea pig for a day of neglect, Bash scratches Harley's furry butt and puts her back in the cage. He returns to the tack room, removes the three bottles of liquor from his grandfather's box, and lugs them out to the Dart. It'll mean another trip to the park so he can dump out the stuff that's been poisoning his life for years, but there's no other choice.

Nehi simply can't see them. Even the shape of the glass is enough to set her off on another binge, and if he dumps the vodka in the nearby woods, she'll smell it out.

He's seen her fall to her knees and eat the sandy dirt where he poured out her rye. The memory, her vomit and mess from ingesting mud, makes him shudder and retch until his stomach aches.

The park is the only way to go. That little trip is what led him to destroy Julia's box in the first place. Maybe Bash should look into homeschooling if this keeps up, since he can't make it through another week like the one he narrowly survived.

And I really should find another home for Harley with someone who can actually take care of a pet.

Bash squats beside Harley's cage and pulls out pocket notes for his essay. It's due in little over a week. If he wants Julia to get an A for him, he'll have to do some work on his own assignment.

Bash grunts at the thought. It's like he can't let her go even though he's sawn off that portion of his life like a diseased limb. He collapses in the straw, leans against the hay bale, and takes off the pen cap with his teeth. A few ideas filter in with the swirling dust in the barn, and he jots them down, words lined up in neat files like soldiers.

The lines undulate like cuttlefish across the fold lines on his page. Bash likes cuttlefish. He remembers watching them in a large tank during a fieldtrip to the Camden Aquarium in fourth grade.

Cuttlefish, what a funny name. What does 'cuttle' mean? The tentacled creatures hang in the water and watch him as he stares back into their intent, alien eyes with W-shaped pupils.

Which one is the exhibit, the boy or the cephalopods?

Bash's thoughts coil into unexpected shapes, float with him around the barn and into the tack room as he leans back on the hay bale. His eyes close.

Julia waits on the porch of the Little Free Library house on Bash's workbench, peering at him over the top of the novel she's reading. Her hair is tied back in a bandanna as blue as her eyes. She blinks as she regards him, an inhabitant of the cage he's built.

Bash reaches for Harley who somehow has jumped back into the hood of his sweatshirt. He picks up the pig, whispers to her, and opens his grandfather's box, now empty. "The bottles are gone," he tells the guinea pig in the silent language of dreams. "There's plenty of room." Harley wheeks softly as he places her inside the padded space once filled with shelf vodka.

Bash closes the lid, turns the key, and hangs the key ring back on the nail in the wall. "Now I'll always know you're okay," he tries to whisper, although sleep makes the words come out as a sludgy, gurgling snore.

His body twitches violently. Maybe he's trying to escape from what he's just done.

CHAPTER 18.

After a prolonged and frustrating through her closet, Julia bikes to the tiny dress shop near Aggie's Diner. She's determined to find something to wear to the LFL opening. Reenie has recommended the store after Julia mentioned her clothes problem.

"Red Carpet has cute stuff, honey, but they won't charge a kidney for a decent dress."

Tom's money is wrapped around the singles Julia won at Isaac's house, and she prays it'll be enough. Probably black is the way to go, since Julia knows fuck-all about fashion or shopping. She just wants to look classy for once in her life.

The days have passed faster than she could have imagined, and already the number in Fry's marked circle is a nine. Single digits now count down to the essay due date, and Julia has yet to write a single word of it.

One thing at a time, Julia tells herself as she enters the darkened shop. It's small but filled with clientele inside, and the man behind the counter flicks a lazy Hello at her as she begins to search through the racks.

There's a line of skirts and dresses on the back sales rack. Julia flips through the clothes and half-heartedly chooses several dark garments. She goes to the changing rooms, shut off by curtains on brass rings that clatter as she enters the back stall and hangs up her selections.

After twenty minutes of struggle and sweat, Julia's found something she can use. The rings slide back as she enters the tiny hallway to check out a knee-length dress in the longer mirror, wanting to make certain she doesn't look like a widow or a waif. The dress seems conservative, with cuffed sleeves and a sort of pouty upper-body thing going on. It covers all the necessary skin and, more importantly, bears a 50 percent off tag.

"You have got to be kidding me." The amused voice makes her whirl around. London stands at the other end of the changing rooms, her thumb poised over her phone screen. "What the hell are you wearing?

Window drapes?"

"None of your business," Julia retorts.

"True, it's not my business. But it goes against girl-code to let you go outside wearing that. What else have you got? Are you in here? Okay." London crowds into the try-on space and flicks through the clothes Julia selected. "Ugh, these are even worse."

"You know what? First of all, get the hell out of my face. Second, it's for the Little Library opening. I don't think anyone cares what I look like."

"I don't care what it's for. You look like the rear end of a hearse."

"I told you to get the hell out!"

"Is there anything wrong?" The laidback guy from the counter appears beside the curtain, probably pulled out of his comfy counter spot by the argument.

"We're fine." London still sounds amused. "Just got an important event this weekend, so she needs something refined." The last question is directed at Julia.

"Nice. You'll need an important piece, something understated but still gorgeous." Somehow Mr. Hipster has developed a smooth manner. "Here, let me pull some stuff for you – oh, sweetie. No." He's seen what Julia's wearing.

"That's what I told her," London agrees.

As the dresses disappear from her changing room, Julia feels the situation fly out of her control. "I'm leaving now," she announces, but London shakes her head.

"Just wait and see what he comes up with. It couldn't be worse than what you picked. Anyway, I want to talk to you. Any chance we can go get a soda or something when you choose your ball gown?"

"I really don't want…" Belatedly Julia remembers something. Maybe London can get the Library Box from Bash, and Julia won't have to write the text she keeps avoiding. "Okay," she concedes. "What are you doing here, anyway?"

"I wanted some shirts, shoes, maybe a purse or two."

The guy has reappeared, loaded down with at least six hangers. "Start with these," he offers. "Let me know if you need different sizes."

London appraises Julia with her usual measuring gaze. "Nothing too ornate – these are good."

"I'll see what else I can find."

His boots disappear from under the curtain, and London points to silk, dark and blue. "Ignore those other rags and try this one. It's the best."

Julia swallows back more insults and yanks off the black garment she thought was appropriate. To her distinct annoyance the blue dress London has picked out falls over her body with a cool swish, skims her waist and hips with elegant flare. The dress is simple, yet it makes her hair burn like fire in the dark changing room.

"Yeah," London says with satisfaction. She tilts her head and yanks at the neckline so it lies perfectly. When the guy comes back, she waves him off. "We're good," she states. "And don't forget I've got a 15 percent military discount."

• • •

Julia leads the way through the diner to what she calls Aggie's secret booth, a seat in the far back of the diner. London sings a line of a song on the radio countdown filtering down from the diner's ceiling and puts away her phone to pick up a menu. "What's good here?"

"Everything's good." Julia decides on iced tea. "But the onion rings are famous. A CNN host did a food feature on them."

"Oh." London rolls the word in her mouth. "Well, suppose I have to have some of those." She beckons, and Reenie shows up with her pad ready. "Could I have onion rings? And a diet whatever."

"Iced tea, please." Julia stashes the menu.

Reenie snorts and disappears, her sneakers squeaking on the clean floor. "What's her problem?" London makes a face as though she just smelled bad milk.

"Thinks I'm too skinny."

"You are, although they say never too thin or too rich, etcetera." London laces her fingers on the table and stares at Julia. "So. We need to talk. But I'm going to tell you straight up there are a couple of things I can't tell you about even if you ask."

Julia guesses she means about Bash. "Look, all I'm trying to do is make it through the week."

"Okay, but there's more to it than that." London stops as Reenie appears with drinks and a basket of bread.

"Eat," the waitress says to Julia. "Men like something they can grab onto." Before either of them can reply she squeaks her way back to the kitchen.

Julia groans. "Why does everyone think it's always about a guy?" She blows at the hair lying over her forehead, flat after wrestling her way in and out of clothes.

London picks at the basket of bread. "Cheese and cinnamon bread? God, I can't resist this stuff. Help me out here." Quickly she rips off two slices and hands one to Julia. "I just wanted to let you know I don't care what you do. In fact, I actually don't hate you more than anyone else at that school. But that's not going to stop me going after Bash."

Julia butters one slice and takes a bite. "Thought you two were just friends?"

"Yeah, well. Guys are idiots. You'd think he'd have picked up on how things are by now, but no. I'm going to have to get up in his face at some point."

"Oh." Julia allows herself a minute to close her eyes against the memory of Bash's mouth, soft on hers. "How long have you two known each other?"

"For forever." London dimples with a delicious smile.

"Anything else?" Julia frowns. "I've got to figure out what to write for the damn essay, I want to figure out a ton of stuff for this opening, and oh yeah, figure out how I'm going to gas up my truck without working any shifts this week. Bash is way down on my list."

"Liar," Ghost whispers into her ear. "I still love you, though."

"Way down the list, huh? I'll take that as your blessing." London bites deeply into the bread and rolls her eyes. "This is too good. I could eat the whole basket. Look, I know you and Bash had your own little library society in his barn, but there's more going on in his house than you know about."

"And you do?" Julia puts down the bread.

Reenie interrupts them again with baskets of food. She's brought London's onion rings and added a few extras: fries, mozzarella sticks, and a basket of what Aggie calls 'stuff.'

"What's this?" London stabs her fork into the 'stuff.'

"Breaded mushrooms and cauliflower. Thanks, Reenie."

"Oh my sweet Lord in heaven," London moans again, and she bites into a mushroom. "I'm coming here all the time now."

The fries are still hot when Julia steals a few from the plate between them. She and London seem to have reached a spiky accord. "Actually, I wanted to ask you a favor."

"A favor, huh?" London pats her full lips with a diner napkin.

"As you've noticed, Bash and I aren't – well, we're done. Whatever it was between us is over. But," she raises her voice as London starts to speak, "I still need the Library Box he built for me. Can you get it?"

"Huh." London sits back with an onion ring speared on her fork. "You can't ask him yourself?"

"No." Julia doesn't add any details.

London bites the onion ring and chews. "This is the best diner food ever," she states. "Anyway, I'll tell him. No promises, though."

The iced tea is so cold it gives Julia a headache. "Okay." Her mom would have would have respected London's sass. "And another thing. Why are you always texting in class? And no one says anything about it?"

London slides her phone across the booth, and Julia cranes her neck to take a look. There's a long list of recent calls, most of them from the VA. Some are from Philadelphia and New York, and several are marked Chicago.

VA? Julia steals a glance at London, still holding the phone between her fingertips.

"About that." London taps the top listing with one perfect, pink nail. "My dad works for veterans all over the country, and he made me volunteer when I was in sixth grade. I got hooked right away on helping former military, it's rewarding, I guess? Anyway, Fry knows all about it. It's why he lets me get away with breaking the rules."

"Really?" Julia is winded by this new dimension of the girl across from her.

"Wish I could be there in person for those vets 24-7, but what can you do? Once summer's here I'll travel more with Jake, go help them out."

Julia's about to ask more about the vets, but London slurps her diet soda and burps. It's a new level of humanity, and Julia can't help giggling – the first time she's laughed since the previous week.

"What shoes are you gonna wear?" London demands.

"Shoes?"

"They go on your feet? Usually made of leather?"

Julia shakes her head. "No idea. I've got a pair of old flats, so – yeah. Those."

"You are not wearing a pair of old flats with the dress we just picked out." London shakes her head. "Nope. You're coming to my house and – wait. What size do you wear?" She peers under the table. "Looks like a 7 1/2 or an 8. Bet we can find something in my closet."

"Why are you doing all this?" Julia asks. "Trying to make yourself feel better?"

"Maybe I *am* trying to make myself feel better for when I take your ex. Plus, I help people. It's what I do."

Julia flops back in the seat. "Don't think we're going to start hanging out," she says.

"I totally agree." London beckons with two fingers. Reenie gives her the stink-eye as she stumps up to the booth, writes their check, and flounces to the cash register. "We're not friends, but maybe we're not enemies either."

CHAPTER 19.

"I want to get out. Wanna get out, get out, get out." Nehi punctuates each demand with a clank on her handcuff against her bed frame.

The metal-on-metal makes Bash's skin crawl. "We both know what'll happen if I let you go," he begins.

Her words tumble over themselves, cutting off reason and rationale. "Think you can do this to me? Think it's legal? They'll find out and put your ass in jail." *Clank.* Her legs piston under the covers, the thin chest rises and falls. "They'll catch you, they'll find out. You're done." Nehi always refers to mysterious beings called They when she wants liquor.

I hate you. The thought sears Bash from the inside like a steak in the microwave, and for a moment he's afraid the truth has emerged at last like a summoned demon.

Blame the army for sending her into the desert. But that's not fair either – they were only doing what they were told. It was the country's fault.

No. It was the foreign government who started the whole debacle, forcing young kids to fork over their innocence and sacrificing their future children along the way.

Or probably it was the art of war itself, twisting lives into empty, broken things the innocent have to deal with when the poor soldiers return to "real life", whatever that is. They live on as ghosts in a society that can never comprehend their experience.

Nehi concentrates on the handcuff, index finger poking at the lock. Her eyes narrow into slits, and she relaxes on the pillow. "Maybe I'll go to this tavern I know when you're arrested for locking me up. Get a seat at the bar, order and old-fashioned with extra cherries. Tell the bartender to muddle the fruit."

A silver snail-track of drool sneaks out of her mouth onto the pillowcase he washed that morning, proof of an uncontrollable desire. Bash watches and tries not to retch. *Stay in her room, talk her down, let her know she's safe. Remind her of your love with small actions: a vase of flowers, a framed family photo.*

It's a useless puddle of advice picked up from various VA pamphlets. Bash pushes off the wall and mutters he's going to the bathroom.

"I gotta piss too," Nehi yells. "It's coming out."

He slams the door on her, thunders downstairs to the kitchen, and wrenches open the fridge. A jar of maraschino cherries lurks behind mustard and ranch dressing on the door shelves. Bash palms it, cold as a marble heart, and peers at the expiration date.

If he fills a rocks glass with ice, soda, and fruit, will the gesture make Nehi smile? Or would it just make her crave booze more fiercely?

Screw it. Bash closes the fridge with his foot, fumbles out a glass, and opens the jar. He spoons a few Maraschinos out of their red sugary bog.

"Drinking already?"

Bash yelps and spins, the jar of cherries slipping through his fingers and onto the floor, broken glass in a sugary crimson wound. Isaac stands in the doorframe, one hip cocked.

Bash doesn't register the mess. He strides forward and jabs one finger at Isaac's chin, the exact spot where he wants to land a punch. "You. What the fuck are you doing here? Get the hell out of my house."

Isaac swivels on his tiptoes. "Well, okay, but – I've got a message from Ju-Lee-Ah," he sings over one shoulder and disappears.

Kitchen, Nehi, and cherries are all forgotten. Cursing himself and Isaac, Bash runs onto the porch. "What did Julia say? Isaac!"

The kid has the supreme nerve to be standing right there on the steps as though he's waiting for a private jet or limo, his lips curved into his usual annoying grin. "Yes?"

"What about Julia?" Bash demands. "What message? Tell me. Now."

"What about the mess in your kitchen?"

"I'll clean it up later – just, never mind. Tell me."

Isaac paperclips his limbs onto the top step and pats the wood beside him in an invitation. "No? Oh, come on. I showered earlier. And I won't bite."

He doesn't get it. Bash is *protecting* Isaac by staying away from his dumb ass so he won't hit him. "Stop dicking around. I don't have time for any of this shit. What did she say?"

"What do you think?" Isaac tips his bright head back against the porch pillar. "What's she been talking about for, like, forever? She wants her dollhouse. Her library thing. I'm here to pick it up."

A scream from upstairs sews the air between Bash and Isaac into something new. Instantly Isaac jumps up and babbles his way to the kitchen door. "Oh, my God! Did you hear that? Is someone up there? Your mom? Maybe she had an accident! Fell, or fire, or worse – a spider!"

Bash slaps the door closed in Isaac's face before he can enter the kitchen. "Nuh uh. You're not going in. She's fine, and it's – it's none of your business."

It's as though Nehi knows he's in trouble. "Bash," she hollers from upstairs, the words smudged by distance and smug necessity. "Get up here. Bash. I'm sick. Bash Bash Bash Bash."

"Dude." Isaac's pale eyes bulge. "Is that your mom? What happened? Should I call 911?"

Although Bash wants nothing more than Isaac off the property, the dumb kid *could* actually call the cops. What would happen if they showed up and carted off Nehi to some facility? Where would Bash go? And how drugged-up would she be when – if – she came back?

"It's Nehi. My – my parent." Isaac seems to wait, one eyebrow twitching, as Bash explains. "She was a soldier in Desert Storm, and sometimes the real world spooks her. Brings her back in time, right? To when she was in combat? Simple stuff does it. The sound of a trash truck or an ambulance siren. She self-medicates with alcohol, except that makes her mean. Really mean. And I try to take care of her, I do try, but it just gets overwhelming sometimes. You know, with school, and Julia, and stuff."

Time blinks forward, and Bash full-body flushes when he comes to his senses. He's in Isaac's arms, being hugged by the skinny idiot who's been nothing but a pain in the ass up to this moment. Tears are running down Bash's face, and he can't stop sobbing.

"Okay," Isaac murmurs. "You're okay. I got you. You're safe."

Over Isaac's shoulder, Bash sees the flaky paint on the porch. *I should sand it and repaint,* he thinks, hiccupping into Isaac's ear.

"Hey. You've been bottling stuff up for a while, huh?"

Bash frees himself and backs up, wiping his eyes on one sleeve. "Sorry."

Isaac produces a pack of Kleenex from his jacket. "Check it out, I'm like a grandma or a soccer mom. Started carrying these when Julia broke down on me a few times."

"Julia broke down?" Bash blows his nose.

"Yeah. Her mom's death hits her hard sometimes. Same with her dad, except he took it a lot worse. Actually, now that I think about it, you two have a lot in common."

A part of Bash knows Julia's mom died, mainly from an overheard year-old conversation. "I heard her mom died in some accident."

"Drunk driver," Isaac says. "She never told you? What do you two talk about, anyway? Or was the thing between you and Julia just a hook-up kind of deal?"

"No, it wasn't some kind of hook-up deal, jackass. We did homework together. And looked at my guinea pig. And I taught her some woodworking." Even as he talks, Bash realizes the whole relationship sounds incredibly dreary. And yet his friendship with Julia was the brightest, happiest time of his life.

"Are you going see what your mom wants?" Isaac jerks his head in the direction of the house.

Bash nods. "Yeah, I should go, which means you should go."

But Isaac pushes the screen door, bounds into the kitchen, and waves at the bloody cherries on the floor. "Were you cooking?"

"Pouring Nehi a soda. She was talking about old-fashioneds and I thought if I put some cherries in a soda it might…" Bash realizes he's babbling. "Anyway, it was a stupid idea. It would only make her crave alcohol anyway.   And you need to go. Thanks for listening and all that, but…" Bash jerks his thumb at the unseen road.

"Well, let's at least get her that soda. Sprite? Cool. Here we go – glass, ice. Now, which way?"

Trying not to slip in congealed cherry juice, Bash curses and chases Isaac up the steps. He catches the kid opening Nehi's door and fists his collar, just as Isaac catches sight of the woman in the bed. "Bash! She's in handcuffs! Is this some weird Silence of the Lambs shit?"

Bash is about to punch the kid, but Nehi intervenes with a sly greeting reminiscent of a stingy godmother's unexpected gift. "Bash, you let him be. Tell him to come in and sit for a minute. I don't mind company as long as he's not a bitch." She drags out the word with a reverent shush. "You can unlock me now. Promise."

Isaac's eyes are huge. "Do I have to call someone? Is there an adult version of DYFS?"

"You try and I'll kick your ass out the door." Nehi rubs her wrist, freed from its cuff, and struggles to sit up against the aluminum slats of her bed. "The only reason I'm alive is that boy." She jabs a thumb in Bash's direction.

"Don't kill him," he warns her.

"I won't if he leaves you alone." Nehi sits forward, extends one wizened palm, and pats Isaac's head. "I like your hair." She reveals white and even teeth in a brilliant smile, a final vestige of beauty that's survived all her raves and boozing.

"It's a pain to wash and style." Isaac sits, all dramatic as he makes himself comfortable. "I can do yours sometime if you want."

"No, you can't," Bash insists as Nehi asks Isaac if he works in a beauty shop.

"No, I work at a diner. So ordinary, right? But I was lucky to get the job. My best and nicest friend got me the…"

"A diner," Nehi interrupts. "Been a long time since I went to a diner. My favorite is hash browns. Or apple pie a la mode."

"You should come and eat some time. Julia might be there."

"Bash, quit jiggling your knee and sit down," Nehi snaps. For one moment she sounds like an actual real, live, exasperated mom. "Who's Julia?"

"No one," Bash insists, but Isaac launches into a long story about how Julia is his best friend that he mentioned and she's so nice, so cute, so smart.

"Plus, she's a lot like Bash," Isaac adds. "Been through some shit."

Nehi nods, and Bash realizes she actually likes Isaac. "Haven't we all."

"Right?" Isaac moves onto the bed next to her and bounces with enthusiasm. "You should just hear what I went through when I first came out. But now I just don't care." He reaches forward, winds an arm around Bash's neck, and pulls him into a practiced, soft-lipped kiss.

"Uh, you wanna ask first?" Bash is about to go off on the kid, when he hears a series of wheezy coughs from the direction of the pillow. Nehi's eyes are closed, lids dark gray against the ash of her skin. The flesh on her high cheekbones tightens rhythmically, a sight Bash hasn't seen in years.

Isaac has made Nehi laugh.

CHAPTER 20.

Julia decides to ride to the diner and give Isaac a night off. His texts have been growing steadily more plaintive anyway: *How's the outside world doing? I remember sky, trees, air. Help I'm trapped inside a French-fry factory!* In any case, the LRC dollars and her dad's money have all gone to the memorial dress, and it's time to earn some gas money.

When Isaac sees her, he doesn't bolt for the exit. Instead he puts down his tray, takes up the back booth, and orders a milkshake as she gets ready for her shift.

Each time Julia passes him with her tray of coffee cups, he continues a fragmented conversation with himself. "Need to talk to you, Jule. Stuff happened. Important stuff. Got gossip... with a capital G."

She delivers a basket of onion rings to him, and he shoots another bullet. "I kissed Bash, by the way. Not bad."

This announcement makes her stop. Julia plops the onion rings onto his table and stares. "What."

Isaac seizes a ring and shrieks. The crispy O's are still hot from the deep fryer. "I just wanted to see what all the excitement was about. No tongue. Nice lips, though. Thumbs' up."

She's about to ask for more info, but Reenie shouts at her to help clean up after a table of two toddlers and a baby. Julia goes and sweeps up trails of sugar, swamps of crushed pretzel and milk.

By the time the floor is mopped and sparkling, London has joined Isaac in the back booth. He waves Julia over, calling her name in a quiet shout guaranteed to annoy the surrounding customers. In order to shut him up, Julia stashes her plastic bin and leans against the booth, folds her arms.

"London's here," he explains unnecessarily

"You're such an idiot, Isaac. She's got eyes." London eats an onion ring and wipes her fingertips carefully on a napkin. "Did you notice Bash was out of school again today?"

"Oh. Yeah." Julia was guiltily grateful for the reprieve. She didn't want to see London and Bash flirting in the Lacrosse Twins group during class. It's her own weakness, since he's going through his own shit. Still, the 3 in an ominous red circle on Fry's blackboard haunts her.

"Did he ever tell you about Nehi?" London asks. Julia shakes her head, and the girl steals a sip of Isaac's shake. "Damn," she says around the straw. "I swear this is my new favorite restaurant."

"I met her." Isaac pulls his drink back, discards the straw, and gets a new one. "Nehi, I mean."

London leans so far over the table she resembles a hairpin. "You did? What happened?"

Julia mutters something about dishes and leaves. She and Bash may not have been together for a long time, but she knows he's a private person who wouldn't appreciate diner conversations about his situation. Instead of joining Isaac and London's gossip session, she goes and hangs with Ben where he's sulking in the back of the diner over a smashed crate of eggs.

• • •

London waits by Julia's bike when she comes out. "Oh," Julia says. "You. Don't worry about the shoes, I got some already."

"Liar. You're totally planning to wear your old Payless junk. Just come over and hang out," London insists. "I have to work on my essay, and you can borrow, I don't know. Paper. Pen. Jake has an extra laptop, so come on. Your bike can go in the back of my car."

Already she's got her keys out, making a nearby GM SUV beep twice with an aggrieved air. The hatch swings up silently at some invisible command from London's key fob.

Julia could argue and say she has to get home, but by this point she's exhausted. Worries over her father and the damn essay have made sleep sketchy. "I don't want to hear about Bash," she declares when London swings into the driver's seat.

"No?" The girl is intent on backing out, one hand behind Julia's hair.

"Whatever. Guess there's nothing left to talk about except Fry's essay. What's your paper on?"

"I have no idea."

London taps the brake and Julia is propelled forward by the vehicle's momentum. "You didn't even start it," she says. Her voice is deadpan with disbelief.

"I know." Julia pushes her hair back and shakes her head, marveling at her own stupidity. "Can't believe it either. How is it due already? Somehow I got sucked into a wormhole of time." She's babbling, but London nods as though she understands Julia's insanity.

The GM picks up a stately pace through the light traffic of late evening. London plugs her phone into the dash, hits Spotify, and begins to tap her palm against the steering wheel in time to the song. Julia flops back against the cushioned seat and wonders how this is even her life.

"Looks like you just became my next charity case. How can I help? Well, we can brainstorm stuff for your essay or something like that, I don't know." London slings the car past a polished slab of granite engraved with Hawthorn Meadows, the sign for her upscale neighborhood. It looks like a hideous, expensive gravestone. "Mine's about PTSD in vets."

"Of course it is." Ghost rustles in the back seat, but Julia is intent on London's profile as she pulls into the garage of her large house. There's another car in there, a dark blue sports model that smells like money.

"You need help all over, not just with your disastrous closet." London's voice is calm in the dark, new-car interior. "We can start with your locker, which needs a serious clean out. We'll work on it tomorrow during lunch."

"What the hell?" Julia twists to look at her, this elegant girl who's declared outright her claim on Bash. "Why do you care? You know, I don't need someone digging around my stuff. I have enough problems without your fake friendship. Fry, the Library thing. My dad. My job. School. The probability I'll never make it to college. Lack of future. And furthermore, I'm not anyone's project."

"At least you know I'll always tell you the truth. Aren't you sick of people treating you like a mental patient or fragile antique? No one even brings up your mom. It's a big, silent hole in your life, and you know what's worse? You've internalized that silence. Bash has no idea what you're going through, and you swapped spit with him."

Julia stares at the blond, careful ringlets around London's face and realizes what she's saying is true. The girl has never held back during any of their exchanges. While her dad, Fry, even Aggie, give Julia special treatment and cover their thoughts with bright determination, London has been the only one to be completely honest.

She's about to answer when the door opens, a bright rectangle with a dark figure backlit against the house lights. "You still out there, kid?" the man calls.

"Jake," London explains. She pushes a button to lower the window. "Hey, Jake. Julia's with me."

"Julia, huh? Hi, Julia. Come on inside. I just ordered dinner."

• • •

London's dad is tall and athletic, the picture of a perfect father in a catalogue or stock photo. He nudges his daughter with one broad forearm and says something Julia can't hear. "Glad you finally found a friend," he adds with a wink.

"Yeah. Upstairs, Julia. Come on." London extracts herself from his arms. She leads the way through a hall dotted with indoor plants and tiny footstools to dark wood steps lined with a runner and brass rods holding down the deep red carpet.

"We can get started on the essays. You didn't bring your other school stuff, so we'll work until the food gets here." London throws a large, leather bag on a white desk chair lined with faux fur and flops into a matching chair, the kind with wheels. "Sit on the bed if you like. If you don't have a shift tomorrow, we can finish the essays and print them out after class."

Is she doing all this just to make herself feel better? Julia buries the thought and concentrates on writing her name on top of the legal pad

London hands her.

Carefully Julia traces around her name, and traces around that. She adds a ring of flowers, one of stars. Underneath she attempts to sketch Harley, but it comes out looking like a demented wombat. Hurriedly she scribbles over the sketch.

"Okay, stop. Just stop." London crashes against Julia's back in her wheeled chair and shakes her. "I can't watch this carnage anymore. You have three days, two really if you count a rewrite and turning it in. There's no time to dick around."

Julia throws her notebook, rage propelling it right across the room. "I know, and all of this just makes it worse. Who writes essays for chemistry? What science teacher requires creativity? It's such a stupid assignment. I'd rather do equations."

London pulls down the corners of her mouth. "I hate those equations."

"Me too, but at least you can solve them *one atom at a time.*"

"Wait." Soft fingers close on Julia's wrist. "What did you just say? One atom at a time. That's pretty good. I really like that. Wait – don't move – here's your pad. Don't throw it again and expect me to clean up after you."

With a dramatic, flouncing sigh, Julia writes down the phrase: one atom at a time. "Doesn't get me anywhere," she snips.

"No, but now think. Fry assigned essays for a reason. He wants something more than the usual teacher bullshit like worksheets and quizzes and Scantrons."

"Something personal," Julia says slowly.

"Yeah. Yeah! Something personal – actually, you just gave me an idea for my own assignment." London scribbles a few words but doesn't offer to show the page. After a few moments of silence, she looks up. "Well? You're a person. You've got secrets, obviously. How about sharing one of them? Fry won't blab."

Working the corner of her bottom lip with one incisor, Julia picks up the pen. The words form as though she's holding a Ouija planchette: *My best friend is a ghost.*

There are huge, cushy pillows in one corner of the bed, and Julia leans back in the embrace of a carnival monkey. *Hospital,* she adds to the page. *Books. Wilma Rudolph. Blood.*

As she writes, Julia remembers everything she's done over the past few weeks. Harley, the barn, the library, everyone at the diner, Isaac, and of course Bash. Even Tiffany's obsession on angels and rainbows has touched her. It's like being part of a huge carpet, one that goes up the risers and is held in place by situation instead of brass supports. Each warp and weft – the diner, the days inside the barn, her fight with Bash – spins and catches Julia in brilliant threads of light and new people.

She writes down her ideas, jots a few sentences. Julia doesn't know if the essay will be any good, but at least the paper is finally taking shape.

A rich bing-bong from the front door startles her, and she looks up. London spins the white, furry chair and gets up, pushes her feet into scarlet slippers. "Food," she announces. "Let's eat."

• • •

Jake stands at the kitchen island, pulling plastic containers out of a bag. "Hope you like Thai," he says. "London, give your friend a fork. I bet she doesn't want chopsticks."

"Chopsticks are fine." She wishes she and London could take their food upstairs and eat alone.

"Manners," Ghost chides in her ear.

"Thanks." Julia hopes the word doesn't sound reluctant.

London motions with her head, and Julia follows to the kitchen table as Jake plops a tray with glasses and soda cans in the center. "Pick the drink you want." He falls into the chair and grins at them with white, even teeth. "Nice to have company, right? It's just been me and the kid ever since my wife took off. But let's not talk about her."

"Let's not." London pops open a soda and chugs.

The food is peppery but delicious. Julia digs into noodles and slivers of shrimp. "What are these?" She picks up a white tube with her chopsticks.

"You don't mind a little squid, right?" Jake laughs. "It's my favorite." He eats quickly, shoveling food in as though he hasn't eaten for weeks. When he spoons out a second serving, he tells them he's been on the run all day. "You'll be glad to hear Bash's case is pending," he tells London. "Your files really helped, although next time we'll need more details for the written report – don't forget times and dates, kid."

"Sorry." London puts down her chopsticks and takes a sip of 7-Up. "And Julia doesn't want to hear about all this."

"Do you know Bash?" Jake's face is friendly, open. Watching them together, Julia feels guilty for stiff-arming London in the past. Obviously, she has her own issues.

In fact, the concept of the flaws in everyone's life sparks a new line of ideas for her essay. Julia wishes she could write it down, but Jake's still talking. "…Good guy," he finishes. "Dealing with a lot. London's done her best to help out, but of course she always makes a few mistakes. Love you, kid, but sometimes you can be a little bit of a loser."

The blonde curls hang over London's eyes. "I'm not hungry anymore."

"Yes, don't let me bore you with my volunteer stuff, since I could talk about it all night. And leave the dishes. I'll get them." Jake rises, a man filled with so much confidence it oozes into the kitchen and doesn't leave much room for anything else.

In silence Julia follows London upstairs. "I should just head home," she offers.

"No! Don't leave yet." London's voice seems tinged with desperation. "And besides, we're here for shoes. Here, blue pumps – no, wait. Park grass and all that, so you need a chunky heel. Take these sandals, and this pair of booties, and you might as well try a few flats as well. Decent flats."

She loads the shoes into a shopping bag from Sax, casually drops a pair of earrings into the toe of one boot. "A bit of bling never hurt anyone. There. Now, I'll take you home."

She doesn't respond to anything Julia says as they walk downstairs to the garage. Jake waves goodbye, shouts for Julia to return anytime now he knows she likes squid. "Next time we're ordering sushi!" he threatens.

London slams the door and gets into the truck. She opens the garage door with a button on her rearview and gets into reverse the instant there's room to back out.

It isn't until they arrive at Julia's house, the miniature teardown in an aging blot of suburbia, that London speaks. "What did you think of my dad?" she asks. "You just have to love him, right? There's no reason to hate him, right?" Julia starts to answer, but London interrupts. "Anyway. I totally forgot to tell you. Bash says he's not giving me the Library Box."

"*What?* Are you kidding me? I just need to get it over to the dumb park for that dumb ceremony, which is this weekend. Oh, and let's not forget I have to finish Fry's essay. This is the last thing I need right now."

London turns her neck to face Julia. In the grim light from the old streetlamps, her eyes look like purple, empty sockets. "You have to get it yourself," she adds. "His words. So, good luck with that."

She doesn't say goodbye. As soon as Julia gets out, London revs the SUV and takes off. Her tires squeal at the turn, and the engine dies into the distance.

• • •

It isn't until she's in bed that Julia sees the text from London: *FYI, I'm heading over to visit your ex.*

CHAPTER 21.

"Julia's freaking out." London sits next to Bash beside Nehi's bed. He holds out his hand, and without a word she gives him more ice chips. "She needs that book holder thing or whatever this weekend."

"Little Free Library. Yeah, I know."

London sits back and crosses her wrists over one denim knee, her eyes narrowed in thought. She's holding back something. Bash has known her too long not to recognize the need to talk.

He could wheedle it out of her, but he's too tired to start. Exhaustion makes his blood sludge through his veins, or at least that's what it feels like. Nehi tosses on her pillow in the hot room, and he wishes he had enough money to put in a window AC unit. He's living on Nehi's pension as it is, forcing a bare-bones budget.

If she got better... No. That's in the realm of Neverland.

Instead, he lets himself imagine for a moment that Nehi could have a few good days in a row. It would mean he could apply for a job with a carpenter or the local hardware store. He'd have money to improve the house, the barn, and even save for some college classes. His grades would get him into a good tech school, but he'd need living expenses, money for textbooks, and supplies.

As it is, he can barely take care of Harley.

None of that fantasy is ever going to happen, and he might as well forget it. "Thanks for bringing over my school stuff," he tells London.

In response she nudges his shin with a glittery flip-flop that looks fragile and expensive at the same time. "Don't forget Fry's essay."

Bash arches his back and cringes as something pops in his neck. "Already done," he yawns. "Wrote it last week. Just have to do a final edit and it's good to go."

"Yeah? Okay. F that then. Why don't we go and hang out in the barn?"

In response he frowns and flings an explanatory arm at Nehi.

"Jake'll come over and sit with her," London pursues. "He's home for once."

Bash shakes his head and doesn't bother to explain. He already owes Jake and London more than he can ever repay, a constantly increasing weight that threatens to drag him underwater.

She gets up and pulls on his arm. In the warmth of Nehi's bedroom, London's touch is impossibly cool as Bash gets towed up from his seat and out into the hallway. "Jake won't mind," she insists. "Besides, I've brought you a present."

"There's no way I can leave her right now." When did his voice become so hollow? So lost? Bash feels he's clinging onto impossibilities, fingers slipping off the edge of a cliff.

"You're really going to make me work for this." London edges closer, slips an arm around his neck. "Bash, pay attention. Are you going to kiss me or what?"

He jumps back and picks at one long scratch in the wood he hasn't had time to sandpaper out yet. "Outside my mom's bedroom is hardly the most romantic place," he says. It's an attempt to keep things light and on the usual friendly level between him and London.

"You're hot as hell and you don't even know it," she murmurs. "Nehi's falling asleep, so we have at least an hour. Come on. We both need something good in our lives."

Bash isn't totally immune to London's brand of sexy. And she's right – they both work their butts off trying to clean up the mess from a war they're both too young to remember.

Julia. It's not going anywhere with her. Might as well just forget everything for once. But his gut feels like he's swallowed a live eel.

London goes up on her tiptoes. Her eyes seem to glaze over as she pushes her fingers into his hair and pulls him down. Bash leans into the kiss, tasting her lips and tongue, before he raises his head.

"Did you hear anything?" he asks. "At the window?"

"No, I didn't hear anything." She smiles, teeth white in the fuzzy darkness. "Just come with me to the barn. We can relax there and can call Jake to sit with Nehi. Then maybe we go over to my house for – you know.

Doesn't that sound good? You've been stuck here for days. You're going to turn into a pumpkin."

"The barn would be good. I guess I have a monitor I can hide in Nehi's room." Bash considers it, eyeing the fresh paint on the walls. "I know I'm a loser, but I just can't hook up with you in this house." Gently he pushes her back.

"No, I get it." London smiles up at him, and Bash finds himself smiling back. In the dark warmth of the hallway, her beauty glows.

"First we can feed Harley a bunch of treats and maybe finish Julia's project. I just have a few more things to do."

A slight frown creases London's forehead. "You've got shitty timing, you know that?"

Bash feels exasperation seep through his body, tightening his muscles. "I made her a promise," he states. "Still need to deliver on it."

"Her mom's dead," London states. "It sucks. Believe me, I know how Julia feels. But this project is getting to the point of an obsession for her *and* you."

He rubs the back of his neck. If he returns to check on Nehi he'll get away from the confrontation for a few seconds, regain the hold on his temper. Mumbling something about being right back, Bash pushes into the bedroom.

The window is open a crack, held fast by the frame pins he devised to allow fresh air and keep Nehi from climbing out. In the bed his mother is silent, shallow breaths raising and lowering the faded yellow flowers on the old sheets.

Bash returns to the hall and closes the door. "I'll just go get the monitor and set it up." He pauses. "What's wrong?"

London has slumped against one wall, both arms crossed over her stomach. Her eyes are closed tight as though she's been wounded. "It's never going to work between us. Right? I'm an idiot for even trying."

His chest sucks in air. "London, I don't even know how I'll make it to school tomorrow. Or the next day. Do you want me to say I'm sorry? Well,

I am. And I owe you and your dad more than you'll ever know. I already told you I don't know how we would have made it without you guys."

She holds up a palm. "Just don't, Bash. Okay?" Another pause. The house shudders with the silence between them. He's about to say more dumb words to break up the tension when London appears to make an internal decision. "Come to the kitchen with me. I want to show you something."

"London," he says helplessly. She ignores him and starts down the old stairs. Offhand Bash registers a creak in the third step he'll need to fix later.

Her designer purse sits beside the sink, its pink leather standing out against the scarred counter. London yanks the straps apart, plunges one fist inside, and withdraws a sheaf of papers. Not knowing what else to do, Bash takes them. "Still friends?" he asks, feeling the weight of the file with one thumb. His other hand dangles at his side, useless.

London huffs a short laugh. "Yeah. Still friends. And you really do have shitty timing, Bash." She scoops the purse onto her arm, opens the screen door with one hip, and lets it slam behind her. The house seems to sag as she walks to her car, bright ringlets bouncing on her back.

Bash slaps the file on the counter and watches London drive away, leaving him alone with Nehi.

• • •

Harley wheeks in the gloom of the stable when Bash inspects her cage, the monitor still tucked in his pocket. Harley's water bottle is full, but he changes it anyway, cleans it and fills it up. He's trying to make up for his previous neglect.

The guinea pig doesn't seem to care, purring as he rubs her back. Bash hands her a few coins of carrot and watches her eat before he stands and heads to his grandfather's workshop.

Pale in the tack room, the Little Free Library waits where he left it days ago. The joints are ready, painstakingly prepared to dovetail together.

He's determined the house will survive weather, kids, and maybe even a drunk driver.

Bash carefully picks up one side of the little cupola that will slot onto the top. The secret component to the house is hidden in the partitioned box, now fitted with a lock so Nehi can't hide vodka inside.

He can't wait to show Julia her surprise, if she'll ever talk to him again.

Harley wheeks again, a shrill whistle, and he goes back to her cage. Maybe if he puts a towel on Nehi's bed, Harley can jump around for a few minutes. Healing pet power – it's a thing, right? He scoops up the little brown animal and heads back to the house.

London's file is still on the counter. Bash figures he might as well look at it while Harley runs around in Nehi's room. He picks it up and slings a few old towels over his shoulder.

Nehi's awake, her dark eyes unreadable in the warm room. "Hi," Bash says as he comes in. "Want more ice?"

She doesn't respond, just waits as he puts down the towels and carefully lets Harley popcorn with excitement at the expanse of playtime on the bed. Nehi doesn't acknowledge the guinea pig's presence, but she doesn't complain either. Bash counts it as a win.

"Towels will catch her turds," he states. "If she pees I'll change the covers."

"There were dogs in-country." Nehi struggles to sit up, and he hurries to help her adjust the pillows at her back. "Filthy and covered with ugly sores you can't even imagine. We rescued a couple. One slept under my friend's bunk for weeks. She called him Scud. Got taken out by friendly fire later."

"Want me to take Harley back to the barn?" Bash asks.

"Hm." Nehi's face crinkles as Harley leaps next to her leg and inches over to her outstretched hand. She scratches Harley's butt, making the pig change from an energized jumping bean to a furry flatworm. The little animal's sudden purr makes Nehi smile, and for a moment she looks as young as a girl.

Bash expels a gust of air he didn't know he was holding in. "Okay. Good. This is good. I just have to go through this file." He holds up London's papers. "Do you mind? I'll sit right here."

Intent on Harley, Nehi doesn't respond.

London's folder is filled with listings of veteran's resources. She's compiled forms, numbers, groups, and attached sticky notes with directions: *Add Nehi's military bio here (see attached.) Send to highlighted address. Call representative at this number before filling out. I've already told her office you'll be in touch, so her assistant will get you right through.*

There are available scholarships, rehab programs, additional medical insurance, even free vacations.

Bash doesn't notice the tug on the folder until Nehi clears her throat. Harley has found a pamphlet from the VA. The animal watches Bash from the corner of her eye as she chews on the corner, and Nehi strokes Harley's tiny head. "Looks guilty as hell." She directs the bright bullet of her grin at her son.

He pulls the glossy leaflet from Harley's determined grip and places it back in the folder. His foot nudges something, and he peers at the floor.

London's flip-flop still lies under his chair, the discarded sandal bright with fake jewels on Nehi's faded linoleum.

PART III
BREAKING THE TAPE

CHAPTER 22.

The number 1 on the board has disappeared. Julia sits in her new seat, rolling one edge of her written and rewritten essay. Mr. Fry stalks the rows, beckoning with his fingers. "Pass 'em up, slowcoaches," he says. Julia thinks it's the first time she's ever heard anyone actually say the word 'slowcoach' in real life.

A messy paper bundle hits her shoulder blade. Amy, the intensely cheerful girl from the next table, hands Julia a pile of essays. As Julia puts hers on the top, an object slides out of the pile.

Julia bends over and picks up the neatly folded square. She opens it out so Fry won't drop the paper and lose it. Maybe it's hot in the room, because the sweat from her fingertip smudges the name at the top, which is written in bold capitals.

Bash.

Mr. Fry tells them it's clear sailing from now on, and they can coast to the end of the year. "But," he adds over a chorus of approving whistles, "we're still meeting in groups to finish the class project. Don't check out just yet."

As she gets up and slides her desk beside Amy, Julia sneaks a peek at London. She's alone with the Lacrosse Twins, who seem to have given up on Julia. They don't yell for her to join them anymore. Bash isn't in class, so London must have turned in his paper.

Catching Julia's eye, London glares. She flips dismissive ringlets over her shoulder and turns to talk to D-Bag.

Julia angles her chair so she won't be able to see them. Amy chatters as she withdraws an envelope of index cards and says she's prepared prompts for everyone in the group. Instantly the other group members groan.

Julia accepts Amy's card, scrawled with purple pen and way too many exclamation points.

The project goes better than she expects. Both guys wake up at some of Amy's 'life-value' questions, and one starts to tell a story about an old girlfriend who took too many weight loss pills. Amy leans forward and exclaims the group could use some of his experience as theoretical background for chemical analysis.

Fry marches past, stops and listens in, walks on with a glimmer of a smile on his serious face – high praise from one of the strictest teachers in the school. Amy waits until he's moved on before mouthing "Oh my God" to the group.

At the end of class, Amy and the diet-girlfriend-guy walk out together, deep in conversation. He's telling her a long story about his bitchy ex. "I can't *believe* how *much* you put *up* with from her," Amy says to him. Julia watches them go and feels warmth in her chest, akin to the comfortable afterglow of eating hot soup.

Ghost would approve.

She forces herself to stand, slings her backpack over her shoulder, and heads to her locker. Everything's ready for the opening tomorrow, except of course she doesn't actually have a Little Free Library box yet. Like the essay, Julia's left it until last minute. The thought of all those reporters and guests arriving to a big zero makes her stomach curl with horror.

"I told you we have to do something about this." London arrives behind Julia, and she waves at the crowded locker.

Julia forces herself to calm down. "Thought you were pissed off at me," she says as she exchanges history notebooks for Spanish, English for chemistry. "Thought you were too busy visiting Bash."

London unwraps a piece of gum and waves the pack in front of Julia's face, apparently dismissing that issue. "Anyway. Your little celebration's tomorrow. Right?"

Julia groans and leans her forehead against the cold metal. "I've just been putting off calling him. Bash, I mean. And now I'm hosed."

London's gum pops as she watches Julia intently. She sighs, holds up her phone, and taps the screen with one thumbnail. "There. He knows you're coming. You should change your shirt first, what you're wearing looks like shit." Without a goodbye, she walks towards the huge double Exit doors.

"Such a bitch. I actually love her though," Ghost whispers.

• • •

Stubbornly wearing the same t-shirt, Julia parks beside Bash's barn. The crunch of gravel underfoot is familiar, taking her back to shining times when everything was possible.

Bash was going to be her friend.

Hillman Minx had agreed to come to the opening.

Dad would leave the house one day.

The library would be a success.

Julia hears a low grumble in the tack room as she walks through the barn. At the far end she sees Bash looking for the correct hammer or chisel. She knocks on the door, her skin prickling with adrenaline.

His brown eyes seem soft with surprise as he looks up and sees her. For an awkward moment they regard each other in spiraling galaxies of hay-dust as she weighs different openings.

I know you hate sudden visitors –

You forced me to come here because –

This wouldn't happen if you just handed the box to Isaac. Or London. Or never crashed into the damn park in the first place –

"Here for my thing," Julia croaks.

"Thing?" Bash's face glows with sudden humor, a shaft of light seen from the bottom of the ocean from a bathysphere before plunging back to darkness. "You didn't have to send your little boy-toy to pick it up, you know. I've had it ready the whole time."

"Isaac is most definitely not my boy-toy." A bubble of laughter dissolves the sliding tightness in Julia's chest. "He said he kissed you, since you brought up the subject."

"Oh." Bash squinches his face, scrubs both eyelids with thumb and index finger. "Yeah. He told Nehi about. Well. About your mom."

191.

"Nehi? She's *your,* you know, mom? London mentioned her."

The dust spirals whirl as he exhales a long breath. "Guess we have a lot to talk about." He darts sidelong look at her from under absurdly long lashes. "I did try to start a conversation a few times, but you kind of cut me off."

Julia shoves both fists into her back pockets. "None of this would have happened if you weren't…"

He doesn't let her finish. "Don't even accuse me of what you're about to say."

"How do you know what I'm about to say?"

"I can see it in your face." Bash scowls. "'That kid, the loser who walks out of class, the one who can't afford a real car, has to drive his grandfather's ugly Dart –' think I haven't heard it all before?"

"Don't you dare put words in my mouth!" Julia is breathless from the injustice of it all. "And do you think I don't go through the same thing? 'She's out of school again, wears secondhand clothes, test scores are in the toilet, uses sympathy to guilt passing grades from teachers, needs to get her shit together.'"

But he doesn't seem to listen. For a short superstorm of time, Julia and Bash shout, hurling curses and their mutual anger.

You suck.

No, you suck.

It's your fault.

That's right, it is my fault because everything's my fault.

They pant as their anger forces them close, chest-to-chest in the tiny tack room. "You broke my Library," Julia accuses. "The first one. It was you all along. Were you drinking and driving, Bash? Like the guy who killed my mom?"

His nostrils flare, delicate as a caracal on a hunt. For a second, she thinks she's crossed some invisible wall into a country where immigration isn't allowed. "Yeah," Bash slowly admits. "I did break it. But I wasn't drinking. Those bottles in the car weren't mine."

Julia tilts back her head, careful as if they hold a fragile glass globe between them. Bash seems intent, waiting for an answer. "My mom loved science," she whispers. "But it couldn't help her."

"Nehi hides booze all over the barn. I spend every afternoon hunting out her stash. If I pour it out in the grounds anywhere near here she'll eat the mud and puke all over the house."

"My dad brings food to an empty room because he can't face the truth. But you know what? I'm worse…" Her words are swallowed in the barn-smell and timothy hay when she sees what sits on the table. "Bash," Julia adds as she realizes what he's working on.

The Library box glows with new varnish. He's kept the natural color of the wood, but the tiny house has been sanded and enameled so the grain swirls with beauty. "This is – this is…" Her voice dies out, because there are no words. Amazing. Lovely. Artistic. An unexpected gem from the grumpy guy in chemistry class.

Nothing she says can capture the moment.

He clears his throat and stuffs both hands in his pockets. "I took another look through the website. They've got pictures from all over the world, you know? I saw some really cool libraries. But I just thought this was kinda different."

Carefully she strokes the sides, planed smooth as water. He's attached miniature windowsills, a doll's door in the larger opening. There's a balcony overlooking the structure, and a tiny person with a thumbnail of a book in her hands stands on it. "Bash?" Julia points to the little figure and raises her eyebrows.

"Thought your mom might like to visit the library. Got her picture from the online obituary… I can take it out if it feels too Barbie-ish."

The figure, made out of wood, straw, and maybe a few curls of Harley's fur, looks like Ghost when she was real and alive. Vibrant with energy and a 40's pin-up attitude, Julia's mom even holds a tiny version of *A Change of Velocity.*

Julia doesn't allow herself to think. She pushes between the old tool bench and his broad chest so she can go on tiptoe and burrow into his neck. The cotton of his collar smells like paint and fabric softener. His hands are warm on her back, the calluses catching on her t-shirt. Julia feels her lungs get shaky, and her face is wet although she can't remember crying.

Slowly, to telegraph her intention, Julia slides her palm up his arm and cups the back of his neck. "This okay?"

"Okay."

Bash has kissed her before, but it's the first time she's pulled him in. He smells of detergent and sawdust. His taste, though, is impossible to define: citrus, pine, the unmistakable flavor of a young and eager male. After all he's had to confront in his short life, she can sense the iron of his will under the silken press of tongue.

If chemistry is an equation, they're solving the problem with simple biology. Julia can feel it, an age-old response to blood rushing through an excited heart, pressing against her lower belly. With gentle firmness, Bash unwinds himself from the tangle of her arms and blinks.

"Wow," he says.

She snorts, laughter and embarrassment mixed in a delightful cocktail. "Yeah."

There's a rustle at the doorway. "Hey," someone says. "Since apparently we're all speaking in one syllable."

It's London, leaning against the doorframe like a model in a country living shoot. Julia draws back, but Bash's hands tighten on her waist and keep her close. "Um, hi," Julia answers.

London holds out a baggie. "Green stuff for the hog. And I figured you two would need to go and dig a big hole in the park tomorrow. And I'll sit with Nehi when you go."

The little bag lands with a decisive plop on the bench, and London heads out of the barn. Her footsteps die out, replaced with Harley's wheeks. Somehow the guinea pig has sensed the presence of lettuce and parsley.

"She's your best friend, right?" Julia asks.

"London?" Those unreadable, dark eyes look into hers, and Bash grins. "I guess so. Actually, I never really thought about it before, but yeah."

"You're lucky to have her."

His lips part enough for her to see the tiny gap between his front teeth. "Do you think so?"

Julia nods. "Yes," she states. "I really, really do."

CHAPTER 23.

"I've got more surprises." Bash sneaks a look at Julia as he speaks. She's bolt upright in the Dart's driver seat wearing a blue dress he's never seen before – in fact, has she ever worn anything other than jeans and t-shirts? The soft material laps her leg, and in order to stop himself from leaning over to feel the warm skin of her thigh, Bash forces himself to concentrate on his words. "One good, one not so good."

She grins and thumps her fingers against the old steering wheel, the first person to drive his car since Bash got the Dart. "One not-so-good, huh?" Julia navigates slowly and leans out of her window to check traffic, since the rearview is obscured by their little house strapped into the trunk. "Not sure if I can deal with more excitement right now." There's a light in her eyes Bash hasn't seen before – or rather, it's an absence of shadow and a little crescent at the corner of her mouth. Maybe she's happy to finally put up the Little Free Library, but he can't help hoping he's got something to do with that secret smile.

"You're about to discover the not-so-good surprise right about – now."

Julia turns left into the park, and instantly the Dart's horn blares in a loud series of flatulent honks. "Woah! What the hell is happening right now?" she demands.

"The Dart started doing it yesterday. Whenever you make a left turn, this sweet ride of mine blows its horn for no apparent reason."

Her startled eyes meet his, and the car brakes suddenly in the middle of the park's entrance. Julia shifts into Park, tilts back her head, and gives herself up to hearty laughter that shakes her entire body.

It's contagious. When she erupts with a loud snort, Bash can't help joining in.

Wiping her eyes on one blue sleeve, Julia puts the Dart into gear and swerves into an experimental left. Instantly the horn blares again. "Maybe we should rename it a 'Dodge Fart,'" she says with a sidelong glance at him. And when he sniggers, she adds, "That was stupid even for me."

"I can't remember the last time I laughed like that."

She pulls into the little bend Bash remembers too well and turns off the ignition. "I can't either. Think we can install it in time before people get here?"

"No doubt. I already drilled the holes for the lag screws and measured them onto the post. Twice."

"You do everything twice?" She glances out of the corner of her eyes, looking certain of his answer.

His thumb on her cheek is careless, lazy. "Only the things that matter." Bash climbs out of the car and feels around the back seat for his tools. "We'll dig over there," he says, shouldering a shovel.

Julia takes the other, and he watches her prod the ground. The sod breaks easily as her slender arms flex with effort under her soft shirt. Maybe it's because she's used to lugging piles of heavy diver crockery around.

He gets the post and measures it against the hole. "I bored a hole through the wood and drove an old iron railing up the middle." There's a long spiral sticking out the bottom, and Julia points to it. "My invention – I'm going to screw this sucker right into the dirt. Idiots who drive the park to dump out their mom's liquor won't be able to take down our box when we're done."

Julia leans on her shovel and. Bash drives the post into the earth, screws it in, and motions for her to come and help fill in the hole.

He picks up the side angled posts and bolts them into position. When the post is in place, he steps back and nods. "Pretty sure it's not going anywhere anytime soon."

Julia puts both fists on the handle of her shovel. The sky is bright with the last-minute fervor of early evening in spring. The house is going to look incredible, and she declares she can picture the books lined up inside already before taking a long breath. "Bash, I really don't want to go and get wasted every Friday night. But you can't dictate where I go and what I do."

Bash looks up. He feels his cheeks bunch, considering her change of subject. "I was never really mad at you, you know. It's just – Isaac acts like an idiot. Sometimes," he adds.

"He's really not an idiot, though. I know he comes off like a flighty peacock, but underneath he's got his own issues," she insists. "Like everyone else."

He nods. Isaac has a mosquito's concept of personal boundaries, but in the middle of all his babble when they sat on the porch, Isaac delivered a few truths. At the time Bash wanted to say, "Wait – you just actually made *sense*."

Together he and Julia carefully free the little house from the trunk. There's a Baggie filled with eight wing nuts taped to the inside. "The online instructions say to use six lag screws," Bash tells her. "But I wanted us to have the best-built house ever."

The project is incredibly heavy, but he notices Julia's diner muscles don't fail her. She's able to help him lift the platform out of the Dart, and together they bring it to the post and lower it carefully into position. The holes for the lag screws, Bash notices with a jolt of exultation, line up perfectly.

Early morning in the park is iced with the aftermath of a spring night. They push the nuts in through the little house, tightens the tiny metal Mickey Mouse ears around the long bolts.

There's no celestial choir of celebration: just icy air and the little house, smug on its strong stand. Julia digs in her pocket, finds the serial number assigned by the Little Free Library Association, and slides it into the holder. It goes over the balcony where the miniature version of her mom stands, gazing calmly at the surrounding woods. The wood plate slides in perfectly, of course, with no wiggle room. Julia steps back to admire the house – finished at last, after months of planning.

"We're not done yet." Bash jerks his head at the Dart.

They return to the trunk and lug the first of two boxes to the stand. Julia's already organized the books to keep order for as long as possible. Carefully they load kids' stories on the bottom shelf, leaving just enough space so the volumes will slide out easily. *A Change of Velocity* goes right in the center.

She touches the spine with one careful fingertip, her lips parted. "I just hope the person who chooses it admires Wilma as much as Mom did."

"Maybe I'll read it." Bash nudges her and earns a bright, open smile. He watches as she kneels in the wet grass, intent on her books, and feels a twist of longing inside his gut.

The top shelf is easier, a simple collection of novels in different genres. There are spy stories, romances, a few classics probably destined to languish as their brighter, flightier relatives get checked out.

A spray of pebbles heralds a new arrival. As Julia looks up, a blue sedan stops with a loud squeal and ejects a round man. It's the mayor of Blue Anchor, a look of determined jollity on his face.

"Hello, kids! Have you started already? Is the press here yet?" the man asks in a fruity voice.

Annoyed, Bash gestures at the empty green around them. The mayor turns his back and leans into the car window, displaying a broad expanse of gabardine slacks. After a minute a woman dressed in a business suit climbs out and joins him with a camera.

"Don't mind a few shots, right? They'll go right on the town website or maybe even make the paper." He doesn't wait for Julia's response before standing by the little house. Bash hears her intake of breath as the man props his elbow on the platform, grins, and gives two thumbs' up. However, the structure holds, even under the mayor's weight. Eclipsed, Bash and Julia stand out of the lens' reach.

The shutter flashes, and the woman stows her camera in a large messenger bag hanging over her shoulder. "Got it. Now we have to get back to your office for the meeting with the union officials, Dale."

"No rest for the wicked, heh heh heh." The mayor gives Bash a double thumbs' up. Laboriously he climbs back into the car, pulls a three-pointer, and drives away. The sound of the engine dies out.

Around them, the morning warms up with sunshine and birdsong. "Um, okay. I guess maybe that's it?" Julia queries. After all their hard work, the mayor's broad gabardine-clad butt and selfish photo-op is an anticlimax.

"Yeah, well. Maybe." Bash is about to ask her out for breakfast when he hears the approach of another car. Bash squints as a squat bull of a man hauls a vaguely familiar crimson-haired woman from the passenger seat.

"Ben and Aggie from the diner," Julia whispers.

Aggie's already talking in a breathless, used-to-being-busy voice. "Hey there, Julia, we brought pastries, iced tea, sandwiches, salads – Ben, did you remember my stadium chair? – plus a couple of friends are right behind us."

'A couple of friends' turns out to be a mini-bus filled with people. They pour out and surround the house, and Bash hears a few exclamations of Ooh Look At That Wouldja and Hey Bennie There's That Book I Told You About.

"Oh boy." Ben edges over to where Bash stands, eclipsed by the sudden crowd, and pokes one stubby forefinger at the little house. "Reading. Not really my thing. More of a baseball guy. You?"

"Woodworking." Bash points to the library. "I helped – well, I built the library."

"Huh." Ben's mouth turns down in consideration, and he peers carefully inside. "Maybe I'll order one of these from you for the diner. Can't hurt."

Aggie loudly praises the library box. "Guess I'm first to make a selection, right?" She flips through the books with elaborate flare and settles on *Jane Eyre*. "Okay if I take this? I'll bring some of my books next time."

Bash tries to imagine what novels Aggie will contribute. Lurid romance? Reader's Digest condensed versions? Recipes? Or perhaps the woman is an unknown genius who studies chemistry in her spare time. Who is he to judge?

"Picture." Ben holds up his phone, and Aggie poses by the house.

Several of Reenie's 'cousins' crowd behind Aggie, start pulling out books and flipping through them.

More cars pull up, filled with kids Bash recognizes from school and families he's never seen before – determined mothers in bristly haircuts hauling kids up to make a selection. Several of them carry old books in their hands.

"Check it out," he whispers to Julia. "Your library's working." She nods and blinks a few times, and her eyes brighten in the morning sun.

A slender figure wobbling on a bike catches Bash's eye. Julia murmurs something detaches herself from Bash's arm.

It's her mom's bike, the same one Julia's been using for weeks. Her father parks it against a Slow Down sign and walks towards her, pale and shining with sweat. "Julia," he calls. "Got room for one more?"

"Dad." Julia runs forward. "I never expected you'd actually make it."

"Me neither." Bash can hear the smile in his words. "But I just simply had to see the masterpiece."

Julia loops her arm through his as Bash hangs back, uncertain of where he belongs.

"Did you build this?" a low voice says in Bash's ear. An African-American woman in an elegant suit points to the little house. "My book club would love to sponsor a shelf. You can put them up on your lawn, right? We could include books we're reading that month. Do you take commissions?"

Bash feels his body tense in response to the request. The lady waits, eyebrows raised. It would be easy to tell her No, watch her walk off. His life, after all, is as complicated as an insidious maze.

"Okay," he manages to grunt. As usual, there are squares of paper in his pocket, and he pulls one out to write his name and number.

"I want this book." A girl bumps the well-dressed woman's leg and waves a novel at her. Bash recognizes it instantly.

"Oh, sweetie, it's a bit old for you. Maybe in a few years…" The lady's hands flutter helplessly around *A Change of Velocity*.

The girl's scowl deepens, and her round knuckles turning pale with the heft of her tight grip. "I will take this book home to my room," she announces. "And I will read it all night."

"I heard it's a great story." Suddenly Bash really wants the kid to have *Velocity*.

"Sorry to interrupt, but…" Aggie holds out a thick arm, indicating a new arrival. The mayor has returned, flanked by the business suit lady and a few other self-important officials.

"This is the young lady." The man beams at his entourage. "We had no idea you enticed such a famous author to see your little library. Box. Thing." He turns to the business suit. "What's it called, Terry?"

"Little Free Library," Terry replies. "Project of the…"

"Excuse me," Julia interrupts. "We invited Hillman Minx, but he hasn't shown up."

The suited woman raises her eyebrows. "I don't think you understand. He's right over there."

• • •

Hillman Minx looks like the tired, older version of the photo in the back of his novel, his eyes folding at the corners as Julia approaches. He's got his own entourage, a woman with blue-black hair so thick in back it stands up from her neck in a triangle. "Thirty minutes, Hill," she's saying. "*Thirty*. Not one second more."

"I know, Deirdre. You already said it five times."

Bash can't hide his grin. D. Craniver looks just like her emails: all business with an air of wanting to complain to the manager. "Mr. Minx?" Julia says. "I'm Julia Cameron."

"Oh." He twinkles at her, shy behind his little soul patch and floppy hair. "Sorry. You know. About your mom."

"A tragedy," D. Craniver murmurs. "Mr. Minx wishes to donate three signed copies of his books to her memorial library. They're in our car."

Without waiting to see if anyone will follow, the woman starts across the park to where a low sedan is parked behind Tom's bike. "Sorry about that. She takes care of me though," Minx whispers.

Julia seems surprised. "Actually, we thought you weren't coming."

"I got a second email from your impassioned young man."

"Is that what I am?" Bash grins.

"It only meant rearranging plans I set up two years in advance," D. Craniver snaps, striding back to them. "Here." She shoves a heavy pile of books into Julia's belly and checks her phone. "Now you have twenty minutes, Minx. Circulate and get back here. Don't make me come and fetch you."

Minx glances at Julia, his dark, sidelong look reminiscent of Harley protecting a ruffle of romaine. "We have to be at JFK by this afternoon," he confesses to a background of flashing iPhones and cameras.

The local press, it appears, has decided to show up.

"The Japan trip?" a reporter calls out.

"Yes. It's a big opportunity, a life goal. Deirdre helped set it up. I know she's..." Minx's voice runs out.

"It's fine! My mom would be... I'm just so pleased you're here at all." Julia flushes.

Hillman Minx ducks between her and Bash before linking arms with them. "Here comes that mayor guy," the famous author whispers. "You know, the one with too many teeth. Pretend we're all in the middle of a very important conversation and can't talk to him."

The mayor's approaching with one outstretched arm and broad smile of welcome. Quickly Bash huddles with Julia and Hillman, who looks appalled by the words coming out of his own mouth. "You could sell them. The signed books Deirdre gave you. They're worth a lot of – oh, sweet lord. I can't believe I even said that." Hillman covers his face with both hands.

"Julia!" The screech comes from Isaac who wriggles into the center of their little entwined group. "Hi, hi, hi. Can you believe it? Press! Local government! A big crowd! You're a success! Oh – *hi*." The final greeting is soaked with dazzled import as Isaac flicks his blue gaze over Hillman Minx.

• • •

Time passes in a blur of congratulations, hugs, and more photos. At some point Isaac leaps in front of Bash and Julia, screaming silently and holding out his arm. "A number," Julia says after a moment, looking at the digits scrawled on his wrist in marker. "You got someone's number?"

"No, not a number. *The* number. Hillie wants to keep in touch." More soundless screaming, more jumping in place in front of Julia's face.

"'Hillie?' Really, Isaac?" Julia makes a face and pushes red curls out of her face. "I hate to tell you, but he's moving to Japan this afternoon."

"Hellooo, perfect boyfriend. We talk, we flirt, we send romantic messages. No sex involved." His arm, marked with seven numbers and the letters HM, waves in front of her face like a cobra emerging from a charmer's basket. "Oh, and you have to give a speech. Mayor Squelch just said so."

"Mayor Squelch?" Bash repeats.

At the same time Julia squeaks. "A speech? I don't think so."

Isaac's pale eyes are limpid with innocence. "What? No big deal, just go up and thank everyone for coming, add a few pithy sayings, done."

Since Julia's fingers are twitching, Bash decides it's time to intervene. "She said no. No speech. Not happening. Go and tell 'Mayor Squelch', excellent name for him by the way, that he has to look for some other photo opp."

"About that. Thing is, he says he'll rewrite the ordinance and take down the library if she doesn't stand up there and give a speech." Isaac raises both palms. "Don't kill the messenger."

Bash feels anger rising inside like a reactive element in a test tube. "No one is taking it down. What's Julia going to talk about, anyway? Nobody mentioned this speech thing…"

"Bash, it's okay." Julia shoves her hands into the sides of her blue dress. "Did I tell you the coolest part about the new outfit London picked out for me? Look – pockets." She produces a few papers, actually folded into a messy square. "My chem essay," she explains. "Maybe I can steal a few lines from there. Um, can you guys just keep an eye on my dad?"

"You got it. Go, go," Isaac prompts. He points to the little house, brave on its sturdy post. Julia nods and marches to the red, blustering mayor. Bash can't hear what she says, but the man seems to calm down as he waves her forward.

The small crowd gathered in the loop of land gradually quiets. Julia's introduced by the mayor, who uses the opportunity to talk as long as possible. "And now, it is my very pleasant duty to introduce the young lady herself, the one who's responsible for bringing the first Little Free Library to New Jersey."

When she turns and a shaft of light spears her through the leaves overhead, Bash has to blow out a long breath. If Julia was beautiful in his dusty barn, she's a revelation in blue silk and sunlight. He's always counted on people flashing in and out of his life so he doesn't have to care for them – or take care of them. But now, watching Julia spread open her essay and prepare to speak, he knows he'll never be able to let her go.

"I guess this project came from anger," Julia starts. "In chemistry class, we learned emotions often come from neurotransmitters, chemicals inside our brains. Anger, for example, provides a burst of energy. Probably everyone here has experienced its effects at one time or another. Rapid heartbeat, quickened breath, heightened senses."

Next to her, Mayor Squelch frowns at his loafers. Probably this isn't going the way the man expected.

"My mom is dead," Julia continues. "She loved science, like her heroes, Enrico Fermi and Primo Levi. She also was killed by a drunk driver. In my mom's short life, the biggest irony was that chemistry, which she loved, could do nothing for her."

Her dad grips his thumbs, two inverted fists like calyx spirals. If they knew each other better, Bash could slap the guy on the back or knock their shoulders together.

"Alcohol creates its own brain chemistry." Julia touches her library, the merest brush of one finger, and Bash can feel it as a trail of fire on his own skin. "It increases dopamine, the pleasure drug, and for some people it can mean a quick release from pain. Anger does the same thing. I've been hiding my anger at that drunk driver for a long, long time. In fact, I took it out on the wrong person."

Across the triangle of grass, she looks at Bash. Their eyes meet and hold, and it's as if no one else is there. *Dopamine,* he thinks dizzily.

She's talking about friendship, about her mom, about addiction, and Bash knows the words are really important, but they swirl in his skull like fine whiskey in a rocks glass.

When a clear, firm voice says his name in one ear, he accepts it as part of this alternative bubbly world where anything is possible. "Bash," the voice says. "Bash." Its tone is low but definitely feminine.

Isaac and Mr. Cameron are intent on Julia, along with the rest of the crowd. Even D. Craniver seems captivated by the speech. None of them are talking or looking in Bash's direction.

"Bash," the voice repeats. "You have to leave here and go home. Now."

He turns to look, but there's no one there. In fact, it seems the person talking to him is a ghost.

CHAPTER 24.

"Seriously, stop apologizing." Julia flicks her eyes up to the rearview, where her dad hovers as though he's haunting the back of Bash's car. "I guess I just don't understand why you had to leave at *that* particular moment."

"I don't understand either, believe me." Bash shakes his head as if he's arguing with himself.

She tilts up her chin. "You okay back there, Dad?"

"Yes," he whispers.

"Julia," Bash interrupts. "I heard a voice in my ear telling me I needed to head home. It was just so *insistent,* you know? And look." Bash holds up his phone. "London just texted me saying I have to get back to Nehi this second."

• • •

The tree frogs are starting to argue with each other as Julia pulls into the driveway, sand spraying under the wheels. Jake, London's father, runs out of the barn and over to them so quickly she has to jerk left. Instantly the Dart farts out one last bitchy toot and falls silent.

As soon as Julia shifts into Park, Jake sticks his head through the open window. "Nehi," he pants. "It's really bad this time. Thinks she's back in Kuwait. Said she had something valuable belonging to the enemy and she wasn't going to let it go."

Bash is already out of the car. "She's in her room?" he calls, striding to the house. "By the way, I don't own anything valuable so don't worry about that."

Julia tumbles out after him, cold fingers squeezing her heart. "Harley," she says to Jake. "It could be Harley."

Jake nods, a grim line furrowed between his model-perfect brows. "The cage is empty."

She doesn't bother to hear the rest or even check on her dad. Julia runs after Bash, her breath a hot knife in her chest.

The kitchen is deserted. Julia registers a red stain on the floor before she hammers up the stairs and comes to a halt.

Bash is frozen by the bed. London stands next to him, her face filled with uncharacteristic fear.

A barbed stream of profanity comes from inside the room. "Think you imprison me here," the woman growls. "Take my weapon, take my whisky, uh uh, not today. I'll squeeze its head off, just see if I don't."

This statement is followed by an agonized squeal.

Carefully Julia edges her way to the door. Nehi sits bolt upright in bed, a ravaged beauty with Harley trembling in her hands. Bash sucks in a breath as beige liquid streams from the animal's hindquarters, and a fungal odor fills the room. His lips part, but Nehi cuts him off. "Swear to Christ on the Bible, if you say one more word this little shit gets it. Gas gear. Chem gear. Full-body suits. You know how those worked? Mask, plastic liner, taped over wrist and ankle. Gloves and boots. Once you got into the gear, you couldn't get out. 115 degrees out there in the Kuwaiti desert, and we had to wear all that protection. We were fried by the fumes and the heat when they torched the wells. Fires lit up the sky like Dante's Inferno."

In-fur-nooooo.

Nehi's voice dies, and Julia pictures the scene she describes, a living hell no one should have to experience. One large clock in the hall ticks steadily, murdering time with its analog beat. Outside, the tree toads scold each other. Bash's house smells like fresh laundry, cleanser, and wood: like Bash himself, all layered under the pungent odor of Harley's pee.

This prickly peace is interrupted by a sudden jangle of digital music. London curses, pulls out her phone, and sidles out of Nehi's room. "Jake," she barks. "Yeah, we need those sedatives now."

When more sounds emerge from the bed, a high wail syncopated with the wheek-wheek-wheek of a guinea pig in distress, Julia sneaks out into the hall to see if there's anything she can do to help. London shifts near enough to speak in her ear.

"Holy shit," London whispers. "Never seen Nehi this bad."

Julia opens her mouth, but stops. Inside the bedroom Bash mumbles, whispers interspersed with his mother's hawked sobs. "Been here for you," he says, "whenever you need. Whatever you need. Already gave up my girlfriend, college, any hope of a future, so why should I give up on you now? You're all I have left."

"I got nothing," Nehi cries. "Nothing." Harley's wheeks rise into a crescendo and, in a dreadful moment of horror, stop altogether.

There are tears on London's face, and Julia realizes her own cheeks are wet. They're frozen in the hall, maybe afraid of what they'll see if one of them moves.

"Julia," a voice says behind her, and she jumps. "I really need to go home." Somehow her dad has found his way inside the house and stands in the hall, wrists hanging out of limp shirt cuffs.

His question is followed by a prolonged rustling and a few determined, stumpy footsteps. Nehi appears in the doorway of the bedroom with Bash behind her. Harley is a frantic and feral thing, struggling under the woman's arm.

"Who's there?" Nehi demands. "Who are you?"

"Dad," Julia warns. "Be careful. She's…"

"That animal seems unhappy." Dad shakes his head as though he just climbed through a doorway into reality and points at Harley.

Nehi looks down, as if she forgot until that moment Harley's existence. "It peed on me," she declares.

"I used to have a dog who did that all the time. Ruined the carpet in our house." Julia's dad smiles. "Is it a guinea pig?"

"I think so." Nehi holds up Harley and peers closer at the pig.

"I could…" Bash starts. He's cut off as Nehi jerks the pig closer to her chest, and he shuts up.

Don't move, Dad, Julia agonizes silently. But it's too late. Her father keeps talking about their old dog. "Meatball," he adds. "We called him Meatball. Or, my wife did."

"Meatball. Okay. What happened to him?" Nehi demands.

"What happens to everyone. One day he just fell asleep, and that was it."

Nehi blinks. She launches into a long diatribe about how not everyone just falls asleep. She tells the frozen figures – Bash, London, Julia, and her dad – that anyone who goes that way is damn lucky.

Dad, just stop, Julia wills silently.

"It's okay," Ghost murmurs. "I think he's got this."

"You're right about that, and doesn't it suck though?" Julia's father blows out a long breath. "Whew! I can't remember the last time I've been out of the house for so long. You'd think I'd be going crazy, but this place feels like home. You know, it's nice. Well-built."

As if she's surprised by the notion, Nehi looks around and murmurs that Yes, her house is indeed well-built.

"Speaking of just falling asleep, I lost my wife in an accident. But I still have a daughter, which is something I forget sometimes. Sounds like you have a son. We're lucky."

"Luckyyyy." Nehi squints at Bash, as if she barely recognizes him. Slowly she reaches out and touches his arm.

"Mom." It's the first time Julia's heard Bash call her anything but Nehi. "Think you could maybe give me Harley back?"

As if his words have broken a spell, Nehi opens her mouth. Julia feels the blood freeze in her heart.

Oxygen. Carbon Dioxide. Nitrogen. Plasma proteins. "That's it," Ghost murmurs.

Finally, finally, Nehi hands the guinea pig to Bash.

For one moment, the group stands like wax figures. Then Bash sidles closer to Julia, away from Nehi. "Don't scratch me," he murmurs to Harley. "Nothing happened. You're fine, I'm fine, we're all fine. I'll get you lettuce in a minute, beets even, whatever you want…"

"I really should go home." Julia's dad looks around. "I mean, my home."

"Home," Nehi barks. "Where's that? Tell me."

CHAPTER 24.

Mr. Cameron shakes his head. "To be honest, I'm not sure. I don't think it's there anymore, not where I thought it was, no matter how hard I pretend." He ignores Julia's hand and peers at Nehi. "Would you like some soup? I brought chicken noodle over in the bike basket."

"Yes," Nehi says. Her ruined face splits to reveal beautifully white and perfect teeth. "Chicken noodle sounds good."

• • •

Ghost yawns. Talking to the boy has exhausted the last of her resources.

She gathers one last burst of energy and looks around the room, which almost resembles a Nativity scene. The woman called Nehi lies in bed, surrounded by Julia, Bash, the girl with long ringlets, the boy with the wide smile, the man Ghost once called Husband.

There's a red mark on the sleeve of Nehi's white cotton sleep shirt, probably blood from Harley's clawed struggles. Julia is talking to London, and Bash is watching closely under hooded eyelids.

"That chicken soup was so good," Isaac says. "You should make it for the diner. I'll help you get a cooking job, if you want, the way Julia helped me."

Bash raises one eyebrow. "You know, that's not a bad idea. Sometimes you actually say stuff that's not complete bullshit, Isaac."

"Cooking job? I'll think about it."

"Hey, how about Julia's speech?" Isaac adds. "You were awesome, Jule."

"It wasn't anything much."

"You have to own it," London insists. "Stop downplaying your good points for once in your life."

"I tell her that all the time," Isaac insists.

Julia exclaims. "My speech. Shoot, I think I left it at the park."

Bash grins at Julia. He leans back and slides a folded paper covered with her untidy handwriting into his coin pocket – the little flap no one ever uses. Ghost thinks that very soon they'll have to do something about the roaring fires between them.

Outside the shadows deepen around paper-whites drinking from cups of purple loosestrife. Ghost watches that gentle darkness swallow Bash's house and the barn.

It's time.

She climbs onto the sill and out of the open window to jump and float, flying over grass and wildflowers. The way is marked for her with glittering stars. There's a refuge for her at the end of Highway 561, a little house where she can nestle and rest at last. Sleep nearly overtakes her on this last journey, but Ghost manages to change her velocity to reach the place before her strength gives out.

There in the park she finds her library where one tiny figure waits on the carved balcony. Looking closely, she reflects that Bash did one hell of a job. Her windblown hair, an old cotton dress, the fierce determination to protect Julia – he's captured it all from that old obituary photograph.

Ghost doesn't need her body or the biological weaknesses stored in blood, brain, and bone any longer. She climbs into the house and curls up in a cozy little space between two novels. It's lovely inside, warm and perfect.

Alone in the dark, Ghost prepares to defend her treasure against rain, wind, and 1970 Dodge Darts.

THE END

ACKNOWLEDGEMENTS

My sincere thanks to Lisa Daly, who continues to be my rock as well as a dear friend. Her formats are the very best.

Connie Jasperson and Johanna Garth offered invaluable insights that saved my sanity while I wrote this novel. They and all the other authors in the Myrddin group are my constant support system.

AnnyM is my wonderful cover artist, and I'm in awe of her talent. She used these files from freepik.com in her design: Free drawn sci formulas (artist: freepik) and Hexagonal grid (artist: pikisuperstar.) Links for both are available upon request, and you can find AnnyM on 99Designs.

Finally, all thanks to my husband. I couldn't do any of this without him.

www.ingramcontent.com/pod-product-compliance
Lightning Source LLC
Chambersburg PA
CBHW071905220626
47052CB00002B/211